BABY PROPOSAL

EVIE ROSE

Copyright © 2023 by Evie Rose

All rights reserved.

No part of this book may be reproduced in any form or by any electronic or mechanical means, including information storage and retrieval systems, without written permission from the author, except for the use of brief quotations in a book review.

This story is a work of fiction. Names, characters, places, and incidents are the product of the author's imagination or are used fictitiously. Any resemblance to actual events, locales, or persons, living or dead, is coincidental.

Cover by Angela Haddon

❦ Created with Vellum

1

ADI

There are three things I'm pretty sure about right now. One, this website is dodgy as a designer dress sold cheap on social media. Two, I'm ovulating. Three, I should not be doing this at work.

But timing is everything for this task, so claims the internet.

I type my name and credit card number into the little box, then swallow hard as I look at the delivery details for this "magic juice".

Eeewwww.

Must be handed over in person, it says.

Double ewww.

But this um, "high quality" seed? It's dirt cheap. Which is a major advantage for me if I'm going to make my grandma's last wish true.

There's a picture of the "seed producer", who will be my baby's father. He looks like a perfectly normal bloke. Sandy blond hair, mid-brown eyes. Not that tall, perhaps five-eleven?

Even though my hair is dirty-blonde with pale highlights and my eyes are a green-grey colour, I guess I always imagined my kids with dark blue eyes. And black hair.

I groan internally. What I'm saying is, I envisioned my baby looking like *my boss*.

Grandma probably thinks I'm going to find a boyfriend, but that's spectacularly unlikely, and IVF is expensive, even on an assistant's salary that is generous by any standard. Besides, the only man I want to lose my virginity to is... Well. Let's say he's not interested. He's a towering, gorgeous, grumpy, impeccably-dressed billionaire who I suspect is also a mafia kingpin. That edge of danger only makes me crave him more.

I stare at the little white box.

It's time. Grandma has been declining fast, being sharp and forgetful in the previous few months, like her mind isn't going to last forever. I want her to have a great-grandchild while she'll still be able to recognise them. Especially since we lost my mother to illness, so we just have each other now: Grandma in a nursing home up north, and me on my own in a tiny London flat.

Maybe that's why the thought of a baby of my own won't quit popping into my mind. A child to love and love me back, someone who won't leave me—unlike my father who walked out on my mother and me when I was a toddler.

Ultimately though, I am not going to let down Grandma; one great-grandchild is not an unreasonable request. Or it wouldn't be if I weren't a twenty-three-year-old virgin with a desperate crush on her boss and as much dating knack as a houseplant.

I guess I should go on an app or something and try to meet a man, but I'm kind of shy with most people. My mum passing while I was studying put a dampener on socialising.

I'd rather save my pennies to visit Grandma and buy more books. And those stories set high standards; I want to give and receive unconditional love.

Not going to happen, so the sperm seller it is.

I live in London. Can we meet just off the motorway? I type in, then pause. I think I'd prefer to meet somewhere else. Not at my house, obviously, but what about one of the bars near work? Being close to here seems—

"What time is my meeting with the engineering department?"

A shocked yelp escapes me as I scrabble to hide the website. "Mr Cavendish!"

"What a surprise, no need for you to jump out of your skin," he drawls in that deep voice, like melted toffee. "This is my office, Miss Blake. The meeting?"

I make the mistake of looking up at him and I'm drawn in like he's a force field in a sci-fi movie. He's tall and broad shouldered, and the suit he's wearing today matches his eyes, just a shade lighter than navy. His hair is black, almost blue-black, and his eyelashes are ludicrously long. He's positively spoiled with eyelashes, plus has dark stubble peppering his lightly tanned jawline today, which makes him look all of his forty-one years.

Still. It's a good thing he doesn't walk anywhere in London, because he'd be nabbed as a model for smutty book covers and then he wouldn't be my secret. The girls in finance and legal on the lower floors swoon over Rhys Cavendish, but only I get to see him regularly throughout the day.

But then, they don't have to deal with him constantly, which probably helps with the swooning. He is astonishingly grumpy.

"Adrianne," he says with exaggerated patience, and my tummy swoops like a roller coaster. "The calendar."

"Right. Yes." I blush furiously as, with shaking hands, I try to bring up his diary. "It's..." I scan the program without seeing. Where is the engineering department meeting? Is it that one?

"Or do I just have to wait and find out who arrives. The roulette approach to meetings today, is it?"

"It must not be labelled, hang on." I'm clicking manically, hardly able to read for the drumming in my ears.

Rhys huffs with irritation and strides around my desk to look over my shoulder. It's not unprecedented. I don't usually mind, except I *really do mind* when I've been doing something that not only I shouldn't, but is utterly humiliating. Sad. Pathetic.

I was looking at a *sperm donor* on my work computer. Not even a discreet medical-ish place. Nope.

I click more, panicking. And then—there—suddenly, that's the right appointment.

"Five o'clock!" Yes. Phew. I'm okay. "Do you need me to change it?"

It's all going to be fine.

Jabbing at the screen with my finger, it's only then I notice that in my frantic bouncing around, I've somehow brought up my internet browser window and it's in the background, behind the calendar.

"Are you alright, Miss Blake?" Rhys Cavendish is leaned over my desk, close enough that I can feel his breath on my cheek. And he's not looking at the computer screen, he's looking at me.

"Yes. It's really warm in here." I fan my face ineffectively.

I'm beetroot. Tomato. I'm going to send the city into a

heatwave so intense Londoners will think they've been teleported to Dubai. My cheeks are glowing so hot I'd be able to get a job as one of those red lights that are on the top of masts. In fact, that seems like a really excellent career choice as Rhys slowly turns his head.

"If the meeting runs on, I'll need you to..."

The air changes. Crackles.

He's seen it. I know he's seen the line of tabs at the top of the window.

Super Sperm Supply.

The little icon is a baby pink and pale blue tadpole. It's not at all subtle.

"What's this?" His voice is hard.

"Nothing." *Way to sound guilty, Adi.*

"Show me," he orders, eyes not moving from the screen. "Since it's nothing."

"No." I fold my arms. "It's nothing. Just..." A joke? For a friend? A hobby to look at weird websites in my spare time? In my work time when I should be actually working? I should get an award, because it takes all my effort to not finish that sentence with something that would be embarrassing and unnecessary. "Nothing."

Perfect response. Very convincing.

Mr Cavendish reaches out and before I can stop him, has taken my mouse and brought the internet browser to the forefront. It's on Amazon, and he pauses.

I breathe out as he examines the page. Amazon is fine, right, it's only a... Turkey baster. The confirmation for me buying a turkey baster.

The turkey baster I bought to baste the magic juice into my pussy.

Uggghhh I'm dying.

And when my hot boss swaps to the Super Sperm

Supply page, I'm having an out-of-body experience. I should check if I can see on top of the shelves, because I'm now deceased, looking down on myself sitting absolutely motionless as the man I'd love to have babies with reads how I'm such a loser I'm going to do an immaculate virgin conception with a turkey baster and a slightly creepy man I give fifty quid.

Blood drains from my boss' face. "You're planning to meet a man on the edge of a motorway and..."

"No! Of course not right by a motorway. I was going to meet him..." I peter out because this is not going to make it better that I was considering near work. Because it feels safe, you know?

"Where were you going to accept this... Product, Miss Blake?"

"Near the motorway?" I don't mean for my voice to do that little upturn.

"No. You're not doing that." He straightens abruptly, looking down his nose at me, thunder in his expression.

"You don't get to tell me what to do," I mutter rebelliously.

"I'm your boss, and I'm saying no." He seems angry enough to punch something. His jaw is clenched so hard I think he'll split his face in half.

"I have to!" I don't say that I considered finding some guy to have sex with and just scrolled and scrolled on the app, because none of those men were my boss. "I have to get pregnant, and sperm banks are expensive."

"Absolutely not."

"They are!" I'm way beyond humiliated now. I'm out the other side, accepting my demise. There is no dignity in this situation, so I will fight my corner on those terms.

He slams his hand down onto my desk, his hair flopping forwards and his eyes screwing shut like he's in pain.

Well. Serves him right for butting into my private business. Albeit on an office computer. During work hours. After lunch break has finished.

He's going to fire me. Of course he is. Rhys Cavendish is the most notoriously difficult and exacting man in London.

When I got this job, it was with the understanding that Rhys was a beautiful monster. The HR person actually said that. He'd made six previous assistants quit, and he'd never even met four of them. Usually the resignation included tears. But I was a fresh-faced twenty-one-year-old straight out of a business studies degree that had proven less useful than I'd expected, and I was a bit desperate.

Rhys runs half a dozen major companies, and the HR lady said he would bark orders down the phone and make impossible demands for reports and sales targets. She said he wouldn't be here much, but would make his presence known.

Ha.

The first time I met my boss, he walked into the office eighteen months after I'd started working for him and said, *"What the fuck?"*

He looked around the top floor executive office, high above the rest of the company levels. When I started work, for six months I'd bounced through the echoey rooms, a single pinball in an empty white box. Then I'd read carefully through my contract and found that there was money available for office supplies. They'd probably been thinking of pencils, a laptop, and a sit-stand desk or something. But I'd decided it meant renovation of the whole floor of what I'd begun to think about as *my* office.

A veritable forest of pot plants surrounds the room, framing the views over London. Mostly I've tended them back to health from unfortunate floppy stubs I got cheap at supermarkets. The vinyl window butterflies were a bit of an indulgence, and the carpet took some careful strategy with the maintenance department and a dozen "accidents" with cups of coffee.

I was, in short, very proud of the office decor he was looking around with undisguised revulsion, and not about to allow the rumoured mafia boss who hadn't bothered to visit in two years to spoil my fun.

It took me an admirably brief amount of time, in my humble opinion, to get over the fact that he was even more perfectly gorgeous in real life than in his promotional photos, and reply.

And what came out?

"Mr Cavendish, so glad you're here," I chirped. "Do you like the executive floor interior design? I've been waiting twelve months for you to sign off on the expenses. Perhaps you'd do that now you've been able to approve it in person."

He looked me in the eyes then and in hindsight I think he might have been close to laughing. Not certain though, as I've never actually seen him laugh.

"Put the claim on my desk," he'd said and stalked into his office.

The payment arrived in my account minutes after I gave it to him the next day.

Since then, he's always been fair with me, if growly and harsh. Doesn't even notice that I light up when he comes into the room, and is approximately forty per cent less grumpy with me than he is with the legal team when they visit from two floors below. He doesn't recognize that I see when he rubs his forehead during a meeting and bring him a new cup of coffee, just the way he likes it, black as his soul.

Actually, he drinks flat white, which is exactly how I see him. Fifty-fifty pure darkness and sweet light.

But I think turkey basters and buying spunk donations at work will be where he draws the line.

He's entirely mute, a statue made of bone and warm muscle.

"I'll pack my stuff," I say in the smallest voice possible. So much for bravery. The lump in my throat is a watermelon. My neck is pregnant and I'm never going to be, because I am an idiot who just got fired from her job for looking at semen at her work computer. "I'm sorry, I—"

He silences me with a single glance.

Yeah. I lower my gaze to the desk. Mr Cavendish isn't interested in my apology. Heat prickles behind my eyes and I might throw up and cry simultaneously. I should be scared and worried that I've lost my job. Can't have a baby without maternity pay and employment to come back to, right?

But it's not that. It's really not.

Now I'll have no reason to see Rhys Cavendish. I know nothing was ever going to happen between us. He's a billionaire and I'm his assistant for one of the many companies he runs. Spending the last six months focussed on said company and all his days on the same floor as me, being my overly-demanding boss, snapping that he needs complex reports at quarter to five so we're both working late into the evening, doesn't mean he likes me.

I suppose this will be one way to get over my crush, but I'm an addict, and the prospect of withdrawal makes me sweat. Cry. Puking is not outside the realm of possibilities.

Rhys is still staring at my computer screen as I rise from my seat.

"Sit down, Miss Blake," he snaps.

I gulp. That tone. I'll do anything he asks when it's in that reverberating, authoritative voice.

Lowering myself back into the chair, I wait, heart hammering in my chest. My mouth is drier than the overcooked cakes the woman in HR brings in.

He heaves a sigh and I look up, up, up, over his fine woollen trousers almost tight enough that sometimes I've imagined I can see the outline of his dick, but that would be impossible since they're quite loose. That leather belt with the silver buckle that makes me think of it undone, the crisp white shirt and smooth silk tie. His neck I have to drag my gaze past, because I really want to touch his Adam's apple and the black stubble just above it.

To his face. Impassive now. Stern. His dark blue eyes flash electric and looking into them takes my breath away as well as sending a bolt of lust right to my clit.

He folds his arms.

"You want to get pregnant?"

I nod miserably.

"I have a proposal for you."

2

RHYS

I should not be doing this, and I wouldn't if I thought my headstrong assistant wasn't about to make a terrible mistake if I didn't stop her. That man selling sperm could be rabid. He's obviously insane.

Which begs the question, why is my stunningly beautiful girl considering this? She could have any man she wanted slathering and begging.

I'd be front of that queue, stabbing any idiot in my way.

Fuck.

Fifteen years as a mafia boss and this is the first time I've known I'm a monster.

I read on her HR profile how young she is, a full twenty-three years. Far too young and pure for me. Even so, the thought of her with anyone else was so uncomfortable that I sent several of my men to check if she had a boyfriend. I was painfully relieved when it turned out she didn't, as I was spared the dilemma of how to appropriately dispose of said hypothetical boyfriend.

So I know that she's considering being a single parent.

And yes, I'm a filthy bastard for wanting my innocent assistant, but I'll do this just for her.

Adi with a child? My child?

The emotions are too big. The possessive, adoring want is a tsunami, destroying all semblance of civilised restraint in me. I will protect Adi and our child.

She's *mine*. She's not having a baby with anyone but me.

"A proposal?" she repeats, gazing up at me. My assistant is so gorgeous she takes my IQ down to about fifty-six whenever I look at her. It's difficult to define what I like most about her appearance. Her blonde hair perhaps, the colour of sunshine. No, it's her shy secret smile that I catch sight of sometimes as she turns away from me.

Today she is wearing one of her little black tailored shift dresses that comes to a few inches above her knees. Her hair has streaks of honey and is pinned up in some gravity-defying thingamy that creates the illusion that I could simply push my fingers into that silk and it would all fall down in waves over her shoulders. I've had to stop imagining that because when I do, my cock goes from zero to truncheon, and then I'm stuck behind my desk while I read financial reports until my erection goes down.

I only allow myself to think of freeing her hair when I'm at home, naked in bed, stroking myself to an unsatisfactory conclusion because everything feels empty except being with her.

All that is to say, she's attractive.

But it's not her appearance that made me fall for her on sight. It was the way she took no shit from me whatsoever when I finally got around to doing a check-in with this company. It really only launders money from my more lucrative and illegal enterprises, so I hadn't bothered doing more than ensuring it looked good on paper for several years. I'd been vaguely aware that my assistant here was calmer and more competent than previous ones, but hadn't recognised how perfect she is. Even if she hadn't been a siren in a shift dress that day, I would have fallen for Adi when I saw the glint in her eyes and heard her point out in the most cutting way that my opinion about an office I never visited was irrelevant.

Belatedly I remember I'm having an actual conversation with Adi. A negotiation perhaps. She doesn't know I love and am obsessed with her. She is not aware I've spent far more time on the nominal activities of this company than it deserves. Nope. She just thinks I'm a negligent boss who happens to have focused on this business for the last six months, in the office every day.

To see *her*.

I was lost the moment I met my girl.

I rally my thoughts.

"I won't have you taking unnecessary risks. As my employee, you're under my care." See, that sounds rational. Not weird or like I'm hopelessly in love with her. "I can help."

She looks baffled. "You'll... Help?"

I'll give her anything and everything she needs. Even this office full of bright clutter and bloody plants.

"Like, with extra health insurance for IVF? That's generous, but I can't wait that long. It has to be today—"

"If you need a baby, I'll do it."

Her mouth drops open. So sweet and wet and pink, it would look perfect with my cock—*Fuck, Rhys, what are you thinking?*

"You'll..." she says faintly, like she can't believe it. Which, I concede is fair. This is not normal.

"Yes. If you want to get pregnant, it will be by *me*. I will be your baby's father."

This moment has brought clarity as to what really matters. Her. She is more important than everything else in the world to me, and whatever she wants to achieve, I'll do anything to help.

I've been holding back for six long months. All this time I've lied that seeing her in the office and being her boss is enough. I didn't ask about her private life, I knew—know—I'm too old for her and far too corrupt for a naive girl.

But if she needs me, all bets are off. The beast inside my chest is uncontrollable. Her being alone, or with some man of her choosing, is one thing. A fucking online jizz seller is another thing altogether.

Adrianne Blake is *mine*. And she'll have *my* baby.

"Should I pay you—"

"No." That's... No. Not how I was thinking of this at all.

"No. Right." She hides her face in her hands as she mutters, "He's a billionaire. He doesn't need fifty quid for his... Magic juice."

Quite.

She looks up, and there's concern in the way her lips twist. "Look this is weirdly kind of you to offer, but you're wealthy. How do you know I won't demand child support?"

She has the most amazing pale green eyes and I admire them as she stares at me, confused. A lock of her hair has worked loose and is partially obscuring her cheek, and the urge to sweep it behind her ear is almost impossible to resist.

Those eyes. When we were discussing the redesign of a product logo she asked me what colour I wanted it, and I very nearly told her the colour of her eyes. Thankfully I remembered her notebook, which is almost exactly the same green. And she said, "Oh, like a soft matcha tea? Sure, I can do that," and scribbled something down.

I have a collection of matcha tea-coloured items now.

"You won't have to sue for paternity," I say, dragging my hand into my pocket before allowing myself to touch her hair becomes taking everything I want. "I'll acknowledge the child as mine." Along with her.

"But Mr Cavendish, you can't do that. You don't have to. Why are you offering?" She's looking at me like I'm crazy and her string of babbling questions ends with, "What would you get out of this?"

You.

I don't say that, but I do say something almost as insane. "A wife."

She blinks.

"Sorry, Boss? For a second there I thought you said, *a wife.*"

"A fake wife." Is that more palatable? Yes, I think it is, since Adi's face loses some of the panic and develops understanding. A speculative expression I'm not certain I like.

"Because you're fed up with women throwing themselves at you?"

Because I won't allow the woman I love to struggle on her own when she could be with me. Same-same. But her reason sounds like the sort of thing sane men say. "Yes."

"Look." She gets up and paces away. "I'm not agreeing, but... What would I have to do?"

"Attend events with me." This emerges easily. I know what I want: her, by my side. All the time. When I have to do activities I find excruciating, or things I enjoy—possible exception on the murder of mafia goons who overstepped the lines of good taste—and her in my bed, every night, her thighs as my noise cancelling earphones. Pregnant with my child sounds like an excellent bonus I hadn't really thought of until now, but hell yeah. One baby. Two. Seven. As many as she needs and an extra for luck.

"What sort of events?" she asks cautiously.

"There's one in particular with some colleagues, rich men with their partners and occasionally their children." The London Mafias Collaboration group is full of smug bastards like Grant Lambeth with adoring young wives and kids so cute you'd find them in the Japanese food aisles next to neatly packaged mochi. "It's tedious."

The aims are laudable—less killing, fewer kidnappings, more cohesive public transport.

"And you think that it would be better if you had a wife?"

Literally everything is better when Adi is around, so it stands to reason this would be too. I shrug. "I don't find it acceptable on my own. You'd come with me and deal with some of the social stuff. You'd fit in. I don't."

She scoffs. "You've got totally the wrong idea. I don't fit in with anyone."

"You would with me," I can't help but say. "And the rest of the London Mafi...Maths Syndicate."

"The London Maths Syndicate," she repeats, a quizzical furrow in her brow.

"Yeah." I thought that was a top-notch save, but Adi's amused scepticism suggests not.

One major shock at a time. That I want her to marry me and have my babies is probably enough for a Monday afternoon. For revealing that I'm a ruthless mafia boss I'll wait until a Tuesday morning, sometime right around... Never. "It's my thing."

Her eyes narrow. "I don't think I'm qualified to be arm candy." She plucks at her modest but well-fitted dress and I really fail to see the issue. "I'm your assistant, I can find an agency and—"

"You're perfect."

"But someone more—"

"You asked me what I wanted in return for giving you a baby, this is it," I snap, then immediately feel bad as she recoils.

She regroups, biting her plush bottom lip as she thinks. "Okay. What else?"

"Live at my house." I crave that. I thought seeing her at work would be enough. But now I'm imagining how this would be between us, I can see that even if we never progress past me taking care of her as my fake wife, and we parent our child together, I'd sleep so much better with her safe in my home.

"As your fake wife?"

"You only have to pretend to be my wife in public." Those words are broken glass on my tongue. Pretend. Public. They're reasonable, rational conditions to make this proposal more appealing. And although part of me wants to demand she act as my wife in private too, there's a voice at the back of my head pointing out that I'll need to remember this is a charade. Living my whole life as a lie isn't healthy.

Neither is eating steak five nights a week, overdoing it in the gym so you can't walk the next day, or murdering the thugs of rival mafia's who are inconvenient, but that has never stopped me.

"How long for?"

Forever. I shrug. "Two years."

Even I can make her fall in love with me in two years. Surely? Over the last six months electricity buzzes between us at unexpected moments. She'll put a mug of tea down on my desk while I'm on the phone and I'll have the sudden urge to pull her onto my lap and finger her to silent orgasm as I finish the conversation. Or we'll lock eyes over an entirely unreasonable expenses claim she's put in for shoes for her plants or something, and I'll swear she's leaning in, about to kiss me into compliance.

"Your magic potion is pretty expensive," she replies lightly. "That or two years of my life are very cheap."

"You're not *cheap*, Miss Blake." I have a lot of receipts to testify to that. "And would being married to a billionaire really be such a hardship?"

"*Grumpy* billionaire who also happens to be my *boss*. And you're—"

"Minor details," I cut her off. If I allow her to remember that I'm a lot older than her, or realise I'm the head of a London mafia, she'll never marry me.

She bites her lip. "Two years as your wife in return for your being the father of my baby."

"Yes." I force the word out like the air is treacle. Having her is so close I can almost taste it. The salt. The sweet. That hint of orange in her perfume first thing in the morning, and the musk of her scent at nine in the evening when I've kept her working late with me for no better reason than to put off returning to my echoing luxurious apartment without her.

"You have to meet my grandma," she adds. "She's going a bit insane."

"Sure." How bad can one little old lady be?

Adi takes a deep breath. Then another.

"This is unhinged," she murmurs to herself. But she pins me with those light green eyes as she squares her shoulders and stands up straight. "Okay."

My blood surges. Six months I've been denying myself, and now Adrianne Blake will be mine.

"I'll be your fake wife, and you'll help me with the whole baby thing."

She means, me impregnating her. Us making love so she'll grow round with *my* child.

"I'll breed you." She is prime breeding material.

There's a moment of shock and I recognise I possibly should have been more tactful and less crude about how I expressed that.

"Yes." And that's when I see her knees press together underneath her black office dress, and hear her breath catch.

Oh... That turns her on as well, does it? Because it makes my cock throb with the need to fill her with my seed and... Yeah. I'm a monster. I want to cover her with it. I need to mark her as *mine*. A baby. Rings. Tattoos. Love bites and clothes I bought her. I want everyone to know that she belongs to me.

"When?" I demand.

"To have the best chance of success, I have to be..." She fidgets. "I'm ovulating now."

"Cancel my five o'clock." I can't remember what it is about. Who cares? Nothing could be even half a per cent as important as getting my girl—my fiancée—pregnant. "And any others."

"But—"

"Now." I'm going to be balls deep in her by the end of the day. I'm lightheaded with triumph, but my cock is hard enough to use as a truncheon.

"Are you sure?" The disbelief is all over her face and in those pale jade eyes.

"You said you're ovulating," I insist. "Cancel the meeting. All my meetings for the rest of the day. We'll go now." I suppose there might be more urgent tasks in the world than making a baby with my beautiful young assistant and future wife, but I'm more likely to be able to sit down and calculate quantum mechanics than I am to remember what they are. Heart surgery? Whatever. Solving climate change? Fuck that. Let the oceans boil if the alternative is I don't have Adi in my bed.

She visibly gathers herself together, closes her jaw that has been hanging open like a door smashed in by one of my overenthusiastic men, straightens her shoulders, and nods.

"No problem," she says brightly... "The *stuff* I ordered should arrive here by five o'clock."

I raise one eyebrow and she colours.

The spunk application tube. Hell no.

If I'd known she looked so pretty blushing, I'd have... Probably not started an inappropriate conversation with my assistant who is almost half my age. It's bad enough I'm in love and have been neglecting all mafia boss duties to play "normal billionaire CEO" with her.

"If I'm having a baby with you," I say softly, "there will be no turkey basters involved." Let's make that abso-fuck-ing-lutely clear. "It will be the old-fashioned way."

Her eyes go wide. "Oh!"

Yes. *Oh*. Many o's for both of us, her in particular. I can hardly wait to have her coming on my cock. I want to see her face and hear her cries as she climaxes.

Then a little smile curves at her pink-bow lips. "Okay. No turkey basters."

3

RHYS

The wariness is back as I open the door to my penthouse apartment in the centre of London for her. It's right in the middle of my mafia territory of Canary Wharf, and is an old warehouse. There's exposed brick and industrial metal fittings. I used to enjoy the cavernous space during my brief visits to the company Adi works for, but it's long since felt too empty. That's worse today. The high, bare walls make Adi look small and slight. Delicate and soft.

She looks around, and the lace covering on her dress shifts. Her hair is a caramel and sunshine, a wave giving it movement even when she's still, as she is now, her hands clasped at her waist.

I close the door behind us and I'm suddenly stumped. This isn't a date. It isn't a work setting.

I'm way out of my depth.

Things I'm good at: managing my men so they are effective in my illegal businesses, killing people who cross me, generating excessive amounts of money, ruthlessly pursuing goals.

What I have zero experience of: seducing women, making anyone care about me, being anything but alone.

What is the point of all this power if I can't take what I most want?

Right. So. What's being a good host, beginner level? "Drink?"

She jolts. "Alcohol? No. No thanks."

"I was thinking more of coffee. Tea. Fruit juice. You know, normal things for four pm on a Monday."

She huffs with laughter. "This is not normal."

And the way she peeks at my apartment from under her lashes when she says that makes me prickle with discomfort.

She's not relaxed.

"I'll get a different place for us to live," I say impulsively. "A house in the countryside with a big garden."

For a second her eyes light, then she looks away. "This is fine."

"Why don't you sit down?"

Her gaze flicks between the breakfast barstools, the dining table that seats twelve, the sitting area with smooth white leather sofas, and the door that leads to the bedrooms. "Where?"

On my face. On my cock. My fingers would do, in a pinch. "Anywhere."

She chooses the largest of the sofas, the one with matcha tea green cushions, but perches on the edge as if it's a stool.

I make two cups of tea, like a clichéd anxious British host rather than a mafia boss CEO.

"You know how I drink my tea," she says as she takes a sip, shooting me a curious look.

I nod, not trusting myself to speak. I have this sense I could break this with the merest exhale. I know a lot about my beautiful assistant. Finding out what she likes is addictive, and I want more.

I hate that she feels so out of place here.

"You should know—"

"How about—"

We both start and stop talking at the same moment. Our eyes meet and yeah. There it is. The flare of attraction and understanding as we look into each other's eyes. It's always like this. The line between us. She's meant for me, and now she'll be my wife.

On paper, I'll have a claim. And I have two years to convince her to stay forever.

"You go first."

"I'm a virgin," she squeaks.

That stops me. Simultaneously, my blood is motionless, and yet all in my head, threatening me to black out for the first time in my life. Well, I say that. There's a hell of a lot of blood in my cock too. Throbbing. Demanding.

I'll be her first.

Fuck, that shouldn't matter, but I'm so turned on it would be hilarious if I weren't also certain that I need far more than her virginity and to be the father of her child.

"It doesn't matter. The virgin thing. To me." She's tripping over her words and she's so sweet and innocent and perfect, I want to eat her up.

I need her love.

Will sex give me that? I told myself as I offered that I'd take her on any terms. The thought of her having a baby with anyone else made overwhelming jealousy drown any semblance of logic.

"I'm really sorry. Don't feel you need to teach me, or go easy or anything. I know you must think I'm..." Her voice goes quiet. "Pathetic. Sad."

"Don't say that about yourself." My words must be harsher than I intend, because she winces.

"It's true," she mutters at the floor.

Then I can't help it. I grasp her chin and gently but firmly force her to look into my eyes.

"It is not true." My voice is definitely hard this time. A command. "You're strong and brave and clever. Repeat."

There's a stretch of silence when she blinks at me in disbelief and I think she might refuse.

"I'm..."

"Yes." Nodding, I encourage her, then wait.

"Strong and brave and clever," she replies softly, her soft bottom lip moving under my grasp.

"Good girl."

And I'm rewarded by the smallest of smiles.

Brushing her cheek with my thumb, it's a struggle to withdraw, like I'm chained to her.

I have to think, and having her within reach and appearing so uncertain tears me apart. It brings out my most domineering nature.

I turn away abruptly. If I look at her waiting for me to impregnate her any longer, I'll lose control and do just that and possibly squander any chance of the bigger prize. A real relationship with her. Not sniping and grumbling at her as my assistant, trying to wind her up. Not being a fucking sperm donor.

I want to be her husband in truth. Her lover. Her confidant and her friend. The person she comes to for help and understanding and affection and love. When she needs something—anything—I need her to ask me before she reaches out to strangers on the internet and buys fucking turkey basters.

Everything. I want everything from Adrianne, and I'm offering co-parenting and a fake relationship.

I stare out over London. The sky is blue-white-grey, a swirling mess of clouds that reflects my emotions as I hear her fidget behind me.

How do I make her fall in love with me?

My mouth twists satirically. Okay, that's a high bar for a morally grey, grumpy mafia boss. I'm not going to be able to jump it.

How do I persuade her that I'm worth keeping around, and to trust me for forever?

One night of sex won't achieve that. First times aren't always perfect, and though I'm confident I can satisfy her, what if she's nervous? She's never shown any sign of *liking* me. Being attracted to, yes, but am I really going to gamble my one chance with the woman I love on what might be a single night?

No. That's entirely unacceptable. By the time I take her virginity, she has to want this as much as I do. There's only one path forwards here.

I turn back to Adi. Her expression has changed to a mix of misery and waiting for rejection.

"I don't mind that you're a virgin." I did not realise I was capable of that level of understatement. It's kind of impressive.

"Right. Good." She takes a deep breath and squares her shoulders. "Now we've got that little revelation out of the way, shall we get going?" she says brightly, with a tone of abrupt false lightness that usually makes me want to laugh. "You know." She licks her lips. "Get on with it."

Get on with it. That is not how I want her to experience us together.

And I can see how this could disintegrate. This smart

plan could be as bleak as London drizzle in January before I know it. We have sex, once, today. She doesn't enjoy it because she's far too tense, but she gets pregnant. Then she keeps six feet from me at all times for two years of fake marriage that bleeds me to death with a billion papercuts before disappearing with my heart and my child at the end of our agreement.

Well done, Rhys, fantastic idea. Eleven out of ten for screwing this up.

I sit down and lean back on the sofa. "I was thinking the opposite, actually."

Panic flares across her face. "You don't want to do it anymore. But you said—"

"No, I'm not backing out." I reach out and touch her arm to reassure her and hold her down. She looks as though she might bolt at any second.

Her skin is warm and smooth but it's like she's made of electricity. There's lightning between us.

Is this...? Yes. I think this is the first time we've ever touched and she seems to feel the significance too, gaze snapping to where my thumb is brushing over the downy pale hairs of her forearm without my say so. Acting on instinct.

I should move, relinquish my hold. But I don't. I might never let her away from me again.

"Oh. Right." Her voice is breathy. "What do you mean then?" Her chest is rising and falling quickly, and there's a tinge of pink over her neck.

She said yes to the usual way of getting her pregnant. She seems relieved I'm not changing my mind. Perhaps this isn't as one-sided as I've always believed?

"You'll get pregnant more easily if you're comfortable."

Her expression goes wary. Admittedly that opinion is not based on facts. It's entirely spurious.

And though she knows that as well as I do, she nods. "Makes sense."

"And if I haven't come recently. If I store it up for you." Good, this at least has some science behind it. See, I can think when she's around. A bit.

"When did you last..." She visibly steels herself. "Have sex?"

Oh, is she jealous? Yes. Good. My little tigress has nothing to worry about on that count. The moment we met I was hers. I haven't been with anyone since, and I'm as territorial as she is.

"The question you want to ask is when did I last stroke my cock until I came."

Her cheeks gain two pink spots again. "Yes."

"This morning." Thinking of her. I have to take the edge off before I see my little assistant.

"Okay. So, if we're not starting today, should I go home?"

"No," I snap. I like that word at the moment. Seems to be effective too, as she looks up at me with those matcha-tea eyes wide.

"We're not having sex today," I clarify. "But that doesn't mean we're not doing anything."

"Oh."

"We need to be a convincing couple for the get together I told you about," I say gently. "If you won't touch me, or if you're scared of me, no one will believe us."

"I'm not scared of you," she blusters, but there's a thread of fear in it. She is a little afraid. She can sense the wolf under the sheepskin I've donned.

"You don't have to be. I'd burn the world down before I saw you suffer any pain at all."

She swallows and for a second I think she's going to shift away. "Well, I'd better get a memo out about everyone buying fire extinguishers, because I'm led to believe childbirth is a bit ouchy."

Laughter bursts out of me. And that's when I know, for sure, that she'll be my bride. She has a wicked sense of humour, my girl.

"Come here and put your hands on me. Just to practise."

"Now?" she says tentatively.

"Adrianne, we have to be able to touch." Am I really that intimidating? I don't give a fuck if the rest of London is terrified of me, but not her.

She hesitates. "You're worried about someone realising that ours is a marriage of convenience?"

"Now, Adi." I deepen my voice into the one I use with mobsters who think they can get away with dumb shit, and ignore her question.

It gets a response. She moves across the sofa, crawling into my lap.

I settle her there and reach up to smooth that stray tendril of hair that has been tempting me behind her ear, brushing her face. So very soft.

"You're going to have an orgasm." I've waited half a year for this moment, for the opportunity to pleasure my girl. "And I'm going to give it to you."

4

ADI

"I'm going to kiss you." His voice is rough and gravelly and sends a shock of desire through me.

"Just that?" I reply to distract myself as he gathers me to him, angling his face, his gaze flicking between my eyes and my mouth.

"No. That's stage one. Afterwards I'll lick your pussy until you scream. When you're ready to progress to stage three—without shaking like a leaf in my presence—and are dripping wet, I'll slip into you and give you all the come you need for a baby."

Unf. Okay, that's extremely hot. Like, straight from my daydreams, hot.

I did not have this on my bingo card for today. My boss is casually talking about taking my virginity and impregnating me in neat steps, as though it's a work project.

And he wants to get to know me and give me an orgasm.

My stomach is made of a thousand butterflies.

Mostly the words people want their bosses to say are, "Take the day off" or "I'm giving you a pay raise". I've been dreaming of Rhys saying things like "Take your clothes off" or "I'm giving you a kiss, my dick, and a baby, in that order".

Rhys for the last half year has been ordering me to stay late, and I've been secretly happy to spend more time with my giant handsome grump. All those months I didn't think I'd want to play hooky from work. How wrong I was. When we're playing hooky together and he's saying in that rumbling voice that I'm beautiful, I'll do anything he wants.

I have about a millisecond to worry that I've never come with another person, never done any of this while he is older and experienced and probably expects that I know what to do when his lips touch mine.

It's a brush, so soft and sweet it makes me gasp.

"Okay?" he whispers as he slips his fingers into my hair and kisses me with all the languid slowness of honey dripping from a spoon. Our lips don't even crush together. It's warm breaths, teasing licks—he tastes of the earl grey tea he was drinking, sharp, earthy, and rich with an overtone of bergamot—wet slides and gentle tugs. He's kissing me like this is everything.

But it's not. When he feathers kisses down my jaw and reaches my neck, the graze of his stubble contrasted with the sweep of his lips sends hot shivers all the way across my collarbone. He must know, hear my breathing change or— oh for crying out loud I'm whimpering. This is a full-body sensual assault from kisses to my neck. Just my neck, and his hand in my hair and on my waist.

Who even knew that necks were super-sensitive? Not me, obviously. There was me assuming the purpose of my neck was so I didn't lose my head. But no. All this time it was just waiting for the rasp of a man's stubble and the press of his lips to ignite me from my toes to my fingernails.

And the bits in between. I'm liquid and achy between

my legs. My clit is a physical presence that it isn't usually. Before I met Rhys in person, I went for days on end without thinking about my clit. It was just folded away within my— wait what is the right name—labia? It was a map waiting on the shelf. Rhys has opened me up with some kisses and unshaven facial hair and now I suspect he has that map, and is going to use it to drive me out of my mind.

"You're so sensitive," he says into my skin as I arch into him. "That's it. My good girl."

Good girl. My brain stutters.

Rhys does not compliment anyone. He's the sort of boss who scowls and says, "That's fine," when you've spent a week making the perfect report to present to him. When you checked for typos three times, he'll always nod and be like, "It's *there* not *their* on page seven."

And now he says, *good girl*? Twice!

I'm melting.

I must really be dead. All that embarrassment has snuffed me out and I'm... In heaven? Implausible, but probably less farfetched than my boss paying me not only attention, but compliments.

Further proof: I can't come from him kissing my neck, that's obviously not a thing, but when he tries to move away, I complain. Not with actual words, I'm beyond that, but with my hand in his hair and a consonant-less noise of protest.

"You like that do you, little one?" The bastard chuckles and returns to kissing me.

There's a vague thought in my mind that I want to touch him too, but all my hands do is hold him to me. Past-me is yelling and bitching that I should explore his abs, his thighs, and his... Yeah, all the words for it are terrible but maybe cock is alright? It suits him. Rhys is cocky.

I'd love to touch him, but I'm incapacitated by how much I'm loving Rhys kissing me, and how even in my wildest dreams it never felt this good. My brain is not creative enough to have come up with a scenario where grumpy Rhys Cavendish was ravenously devouring me faster than I can figure out where I want to explore him.

But however much I'm enjoying him sending forked lightning over my body with kisses to my neck, I can't keep him there. Rhys works patiently down. He is stronger than me and my boss, and that is how I account for the residual obedience. I don't stop him. He reaches the neckline of my dress, growling when the stiff fabric won't yield and allow him to access the swell of my breasts.

"You don't have—"

I'm cut off by Rhys jerking the shoulders of the dress down to my elbows, pinning my arms in place. I'm wearing a soft bralette since I have breasts that are more tangerines than melons. So when Rhys pushes down my dress it goes too, and I'm utterly exposed, and set aflame. I let out a squeak of surprise and he raises his head and pins me with his midnight-blue eyes.

Whatever he sees in my face makes him hide a pleased smile as he lowers his head again. "Lean back."

He holds my waist, my arms are trapped by the shoulder straps, and it's utter trust to fall onto the sofa, Rhys' grip still tight on me.

"So responsive, I bet you'll be even more so when I come inside you," he mutters, then my brain goes to mush as his mouth finds my nipple. When his lips touch me there, I discover he's right. This feels much better.

I'm not really in control of the situation and if I tried to move I think I'd flounder like a chubby seal cub on the beach.

But with Rhys touching me, I don't care. And I've never felt this good before. He is working utter magic. Have all the nerve endings on my skin always been connected to each other, with pleasure in one place firing off a chain reaction of delicious sensations? I presume Rhys hasn't completely altered my biology with the simple expedient of... I lose my train of thought as he gently bites my breast. *Bites*. I didn't know I liked being bitten.

But as he kisses down my torso, still covered with my dress, I think perhaps he has changed me. I guess he will, what with getting me pregnant. But already I feel more vibrant. Like someone turned up the sun.

He drags the skirt of my dress up. No asking, no "Please can I touch you?". Rhys is the same here as he is at work. He's decided he knows best, and he's doing that.

Then he's on his knees before me. My actual boss, this six-foot-three wall of muscle and testosterone, is kneeling at my feet.

"Lift your hips," he orders as he looks at the plain white cotton knickers he's revealed.

There isn't time or space to be embarrassed about my underwear, because as soon as I move my hips, he's tugged it down my legs and slips off my shoes too.

He cups my thighs and holds my eyes with his as he pushes my knees apart, then slowly, deliberately eases his gaze down.

"You're wet."

I chomp down on my lip to prevent myself from apologising.

"Is all that lovely cream for me, sweetheart?" His voice is gravelly as he lowers his head. I've never heard him speak like this.

I nod, but that's not enough for him, as his breath ghosts

over where I'm throbbing with need and he says, "Words. Use your words."

"Yes," I gasp out. "Yes, it's for you. You did that to me."

He hums with agreement and around his eyes creases in an almost smile. "I knew you'd be my good girl."

Then he licks. A confident stroke this time, and I moan.

Is that really what I had to do to gain his approval? Let him taste me? Hell, if I'd known, I'd have jumped onto his desk and pulled up my skirt the first time he arrived in the office. I'd have been haranguing him about being an absent boss for a year and a half.

I have just enough presence of mind to watch him. I meet Rhys' navy eyes looking back at me. They're intense and hooded and he's watching my every expression as he drives me wild. He lifts his head the smallest amount, like it's painful to tear himself away but he must savour this, and runs his tongue over his lips. "You taste delicious."

I don't even have a chance to answer because he... Was that his teeth? Who knows, but all the air has gone from my lungs. I'm lightheaded, and every part of my attention is on my clit where he's doing something specular with his mouth.

Then he licks me again, and again, harder and longer and I think he's sucking at me as I pant and writhe. My breasts are still exposed and my nipples are hard. Fabric is rucked around my waist, since this shift dress isn't floaty and easy access.

But Rhys doesn't seem to care about any of that, so neither do I. He shifts slightly and there's a touch below where he's laving my clit.

It's gentle, questioning. Then I let out a whimper as the tip of his finger slides into me, and then it's not. He's firm and almost demanding as he strokes me from the inside out, and perhaps I'm not dextrous enough or my fingers aren't as big as his, but it feels superb. After all his patient building, I'm right on the edge. He seems to know, as he pushes me higher, stroking me faster and a bit rough, like he's as unravelled by this as I am.

"That's it, come on my tongue. And my fingers." His voice is muffled and thick as he doesn't take his mouth from me. Apparently there are duelling needs in him—to talk dirty to me and do indescribably filthy things between my legs. "You feel so good."

I'm his toy, I think vaguely, as I spin out of control. I clutch at nothing and everything. Maybe the sofa, possibly Rhys, could be the ceiling for all I know, as I'm wracked by my orgasm. The pleasure goes right down to my toes, so intense and powerful I've never been so satisfied or desperate for more. As soon as the peak crests I want it back again, and Rhys, sweet good man that he is, eases me through the stars and fireworks going off in my body.

He continues to pump his fingers—apparently plural now—into my passage, but has moved to kissing over my clit. And he's saying things. Words I can barely hear through the ringing in my ears and the thrum of my blood.

That I'm good. I'm even better than he imagined. He can't wait to feel me around his cock because I was made for him, that my body is more beautiful than he thought and he wants to see me naked and coming on his face again.

Wait, than he imagined? He imagined this?

"Caught you at last," Rhys whispers against my inner thigh, and that, I'm sure I was not supposed to hear, as he sits back then and says, "Okay?"

Better than okay.

Amazing.

His mouth is shiny, and so are his cheeks. He watches

me with glittering eyes like the night sky—I think I'm gaping like a fish—as he brushes his thumb over the wet patches of his stubbly cheeks and then slides it and his first two fingers into his mouth and sucks them clean.

I have never seen anything as hot in my entire, apparently very sheltered life, as this beautiful man enjoying the taste of the cream from my pussy.

"It was good." That's the best adjective I can think of. My brain cells are destroyed. "Was it okay for you?"

His slow smirk is answer enough. "You did really well, sweetheart. But we need more practice before I breed you."

Oh my god.

I nod eagerly. Yep. Quite happy to repeat that.

"Every night," he adds.

"Every night?" I echo, my mind not functioning yet. Oh yeah, a month of him doing that to me? I'd sign any contract. All the prenups, NDAs by the dozen.

"Just so you're completely comfortable with me when we meet the London maths bosses. And when next month..."

I'm still nodding while I remember this is all a sham. He's doing this so I'll be a convincing fake wife, and when we do have sex, I'll get pregnant.

Because it's then the full meaning of his words hits me. We're not going to have sex for a month but he's going to make me come.

And I won't be allowed to make him come.

This is going to be torture...

5

RHYS

I stare at the market projections report on my desk and wonder if it would be excessive to have the interior decorator I hired last year killed. She insisted on arranging a spare room in my apartment. Said I'd be glad I had it sooner or later.

I am not glad.

I am tired and fractious as a toddler. Or a mafia boss thwarted by his own idiotic insistence on keeping his word.

Fucks sake. Hasn't it all gone too far when a kingpin has to abide by the deals he himself made less than twenty-four hours ago?

So unreasonable.

Last night I barely slept. Having Adi so close and yet so far was torture and it was all because of that ill-conceived spare room. If there had only been one bed Adi would have been in my arms all night.

I still wouldn't have slept, obviously. But I would have had her skin next to mine, her scent over me, her hair tickling my chin. I would, in short, have had Adi close and that might have filled the cavernous hole in my chest.

Now I know how she tastes—sweet and salt and musky—I can't wait to have her coming again. But I'm as stupid as a newly-minted goon in a third tier outer London mafia.

This bargain? A whole month of this before I can have her? It's going to be hard.

Literally.

My cock has been aching since the moment she accepted my offer. It's mildly amazing I have blood anywhere else in my body given how much seems to be pulsing at my groin.

Seeing her in the morning at the breakfast table, still a bit rumpled and sleepy, was a special kind of torture. She was so incredibly sweet as she stumbled around looking for sustenance. My girl does not wake up without a milky coffee and three slices of toast swimming in butter and strawberry jam.

She let me take her hand as we left the building, and I probably held her a bit too tight on the journey to work, but there was no way I was going to relinquish the soft little paw in mine.

Now she's in the vestibule office attached to this one. Alone. My desk is set back, so I can't see her.

What if she's having second thoughts? She could be swiping on an app, or logging back into that chat with Mr super spunk seller.

Totally unacceptable. We should just get married today. Then there will be no question that she's mine, going to have my baby, and I'm in this. But I told her this morning over breakfast to plan the wedding however she likes, to spare no expense. Even I know that weddings are a big deal for the bride. Me? I wouldn't care about getting married in a cardboard box so long as at the end of it I could call her my wife, and she remained at my side and happy for eternity.

But what if she's getting her hopes up about something totally unsuitable, like a wedding next summer? A wedding after she's pregnant, perhaps? Or worse still, after it's born, so the baby wouldn't have my surname. So *Adi* wouldn't have that signifier that she's mine.

Oh crap. I didn't think this through.

"Adi," I bark into the phone that connects to hers. "Come in here."

"Yes Mr Cavendish," she says, then drops the call before I can say anything else.

The fuck?

She has a sunny smile when she walks through the open sliding doors, and I'm blinded. I saw her this morning. I held her hand, and yet she might as well be the sun as I'm thrown out of a dark cave into the light.

"Rhys," I grumble. "Call me Rhys."

"You're my boss. Mr Cavendish." She blinks innocently.

I sigh. "Where are you at with the wedding planning? If we brought it forwards would that be an issue?"

She tilts her head. "What wedding planning?"

"The wedding planning you've been doing this morning," I say with a touch of impatience. "If we just missed all of the..." I circle my hand in the air to indicate... I don't know. Sugared almonds and women in hats? "If we got married this afternoon, would that be an issue for what you've already planned?"

"I have been replying to emails this morning, because we're at work. That is what you pay me to do," she points out in an infuriatingly reasonable tone.

"Didn't stop you with the jizz procurement yesterday," I point out.

Two red spots appear on her cheekbones. "Yes. Well.

I'm sorry about that. I'm trying to make up for it by being extra productive in my job today, Mr Cavendish."

"Rhys. And your job is to be my wife."

"For crying out loud," she says under her breath. "I am not yet your wife. I am your assistant."

"And I have told you—remedy that."

"Do not scowl at me for doing my job, Mr Cavendish."

I'm not—alright I probably am scowling. With good reason. She's got the priorities all mixed up. The emails? Fuck the emails. Our wedding is the only important thing. I open my mouth to point out this is a company for money laundering, and none of the business matters, but then shut it.

Hmm.

Right. I was generally intending for her not to hear about my mafia goings-on.

"No more emails," I say instead. "We're taking the rest of the day off."

"But I have to work," she insists. "That's what you pay me for."

"Nope. From now on, I pay you to arrange our wedding and have our baby. And we're getting married this afternoon."

"You can't—"

"Sit down." My tone must be as dark as I feel, since she clenches her teeth but does as I order.

"The wedding. Have you thought about it?"

She swallows and wobbles her head in that way that says, *yes,* but also *no,* and mainly *I don't want to confess any of this.*

"What does our wedding look like, Adi," I say more gently. "Tell me what you'd like. Diamond ring? Big white dress?" I grasp around, basically doing word association with wedding like I'm in a nineties daytime television game show.

"I don't need any of that," she says in a small voice. "I just wish…"

"What?" I demand.

She smooths her hands over her skirt. Those prissy suit-dresses she wears really do it for me.

"I wish my grandmother could be at our wedding," she says matter-of-factly. "But she can't."

"Why can't she?"

"She can't get out of bed. And she's been going a bit loopy. That's why I have to get pregnant quickly. Before she gets worse." Adi's mouth turns down at the corners. "And no, we can't video call her or whatever. She hates all of that. Won't even speak to me on the phone." She tries for a laugh, but it sounds far sadder than I think she'd like me to have heard.

I'm glad I did.

Nothing else matters to me other than Adi's happiness. If our wedding being attended by her grandmother is important to her, then it's what will happen. Honestly, who cares about where we get married. The only point of this for me is that she'll be my *wife*.

"If she can't get out of bed, we'll go to her."

"That's sweet." She gives me a tepid smile. "But a visit afterwards isn't the same thing, is it?"

"Not afterwards. We'll get married wherever she is. In her bedroom, if need be."

"You. A billionaire. Getting married in a care home up north," she huffs sceptically. "And I don't think it's even possible. Definitely not today."

"For a woman who renovated the whole executive office

floor without her boss knowing, you are remarkably lacking in imagination."

She looks askance at me. "What do you mean?"

"I mean we have work to do, little one."

Adi is a bit scared by the helicopter, which is fine by me as she sneaks close as we take off, and when I slide an arm over her shoulders she eagerly snuggles in. I breathe in the scent of her. Cherries. So sweet.

There's too much noise to talk as we travel north to her grandmother.

I honestly don't know what to expect when we're set down on the lawn of the care home. All I did was snatch the phone from Adi when she'd found someone local and kept saying higher numbers until they agreed to drop everything and organise the wedding. But Adi's gasp is expressive enough as we walk, my arm still around her waist because I'm a possessive psychopath, towards a walled garden with a large terrace.

Close to fifty older adults are sitting in curved rows facing a gazebo. As we go through the archway into the garden they break into applause and next to me in her white dress, Adi gapes and blushes.

That blush suits her, and I smile.

"Rhys," she breathes. "How did all this happen?"

It's a riot of colour. The florist has excelled herself. She obviously didn't have enough white flowers, or even flowers of one colour, so the terrace is coated with petals in a rainbow of hues, one into another, in patches. The gazebo looks like it's made of flowers, mainly pale pastels compared to the more vibrant colours underfoot as we walk to the front where there is an officiant waiting.

Adi's dress parts the flowers on the ground. It's long and white and not as clingy to her perfect curves as I would have chosen for her, but her eyes shone when she saw it.

There's applause, mainly from the care home staff scattered among the residents, as we approach.

"Grandma!" Adi lets out a little shriek of delight as she sees a woman in a chunky high-backed chair at the front.

"Go to her." I relinquish my hold but Adi doesn't, dragging me with her to her grandmother's side. Then they're hugging and my heart squeezes at seeing my girl so happy.

"Are you going to introduce me to your young man?" her grandmother asks, with a sardonic slant of an eyebrow.

"This is Rhys Cavendish," she says, a bit shyly.

"A pleasure to meet you, Mrs Blake." I give her what I hope is an ingratiating smile. I've never tried one before, so I shouldn't be surprised when she looks down her nose at me, despite my standing over her. She has grey hair in a little bun and is wearing a scoop neck top and cardigan.

"I'm chucked all of a heap..." she says conspiratorially to Adi. "Where did you find this fine specimen?"

"Ah..." Adi meets my eyes and panic flares in hers. "He's er..."

"We met at work."

"Wouldn't mind coming out of retirement if that's the sort of men available in the workplace, nowadays," Adi's grandmother says, at full volume, to the woman next to her with white hair and dark skin who must be her friend.

"Let me look at you," she demands. I step forward obediently. "Phssh, you're up in the sky. Think I can get up a ladder to see you? Down here." She flaps her hand to indicate I should come to her level.

As I kneel, Adi smothers a mortified laugh and says, "Grandma!"

Mrs Blake examines me, finger to my jaw, turning my head to and fro. "Hmmm. You could cut yourself on these cheekbones."

"Daily problem," I agree. "I sand them with a file."

Her friend laughs openly at my joke and to the side, the officiant looks nervously between Adi and me. Mrs Blake isn't amused, and glares at everyone, haughty as a queen.

"What makes you think you're good enough for my granddaughter?"

"That's not the case!" Adi puts her hand on my shoulder, and I don't allow that moment to pass by.

I grab and hold it there, stroking my thumb over her knuckles reassuringly.

"Rhys is—"

"I'm not good enough for your granddaughter. But I'll try." I might be a billionaire mafia boss CEO, but she is clever and sweet and sexy and a whizz with digital presentation software.

Mrs Blake scoffs. "Has he put a bun in your oven, Adi? Is that why you're marrying him? A bit old-fashioned, isn't it?"

Adi groans and puts her hands over her face.

I stand, grinning, and pull Adi to my side. She fits right under my arm and her hand wraps around my waist, holding me like I might run away after being grilled by her grandmother.

Ha. Matriarchs are frightening, but not as scary as me.

"Not yet. But we're going to get the heat cranked up and make some dough, don't worry."

"Well, I can see he's handsome and has a few bob to spare. But is he kind? Hmm?" Mrs Blake seems to expect a reply, staring at me beadily even as she talks about me not to me, but doesn't leave me space to answer. "Will he be a good father? Can he look after you?"

"I'll make it my life's mission to ensure your granddaughter's happiness."

The smallest smile stretches Mrs Blake's mouth and her eyes twinkle. "You've made such a palaver now, better finish the show."

And that's it, we're dismissed.

"Sorry. I'm so sorry," Adi whispers as I lead her to the little platform in the gazebo where the officiant is waiting, bemused and doing a decent job of hiding it. "She's so much more rational than when I last saw her. Maybe she just had a temporary lapse. I had no idea she'd grill you."

"If I were twenty years younger..." Mrs Blake's voice rings out behind us, and I catch Adi's eye as we both splutter with laughter.

"Don't be." I take Adi's hands in mine. "I like her. She loves you and wants to protect you." We have that in common. "I think we'll get on just fine."

The officiant coughs subtly and the urge to kiss Adi's nerves away is almost irresistible. But I haven't got where I am by being anything less than patient.

"I'm going to marry you now." I lean forward to breathe into her ear. "And later, I will push that white silk up your thighs and eat my wife's pussy."

She lets out a tiny whimper, but as I straighten to my full height, Adi nods, eyes sparkling.

6

ADI

I am fake married to my billionaire boss.

Well, the relationship is fake, not the marriage, that's real. I have witnesses and a certificate and everything. The boss bit isn't false.

Gah.

I'm losing track of what's real and what's a charade and what is just my wishful thinking.

As I work at my desk, a week later, blurred memories of our wedding day pop into my mind occasionally, like a half-remembered dream. The way he cupped my head and looked into my eyes when the officiant said, "You may kiss the bride". The sweep of his palm over my cheek and the tender warmth of his lips. How he stayed by my side for the rest of the afternoon. The way the day stretched out, and a band appeared from nowhere. Granny flirted outrageously with Rhys, who smiled and winked back.

He is an outstanding actor, my husband. So charming when he wants to be, my grumpy boss.

As I work on a financial statement, I remember our wedding day turning from white-gold to pink to purple, then the moon came out and just a few stalwarts—including a suave gentleman with a crooked bow tie drinking champagne with one of Rhys' bodyguards.

Rhys was as good as his word. Or threat. My terror of the helicopter on the second occasion was only three-quarters real, but Rhys' protectiveness was too delicious to be stoic about my fear. Even though it was late by the time we arrived home—I mean back to his place—Rhys pushed me against that exposed brick wall and ordered me to lift my skirts in a low growl that shot arousal right to my core. Then he ate my pussy like he'd been thinking of nothing else all day. He even caught me when my knees gave way as I came, sweeping me into his arms and carrying me to my bedroom, before leaving me... Alone.

And that's been the pattern for the last week.

It's the reverse of the previous six months. Instead of piling work on me at ten to five, he has been finding excuses to leave the office earlier and earlier. If I didn't know what an astounding liar he is—London Maths Syndicate indeed—I'd think he was looking forward to getting me half naked and fully boneless every afternoon.

I guess it's only been a week. He takes responsibilities seriously, that's all. I'm certain I'm going to break him down and he'll let me touch him. But so far—nada.

Not no erection. He's hard so often I'm slightly concerned about his blood pressure. Wouldn't look good to marry a billionaire and then have him die of an arousal-induced heart attack shortly afterwards. Wouldn't go down well with the police.

Yeah, that's the reason I'm obsessed with touching his cock and making him come for me. Absolutely. Only that. Don't want to be arrested.

And I think the tension is getting to him too. Today he's

been more fractious than usual. He snapped at the HR team and has been massaging his forehead since we arrived in the office at eight. I'm going to have to relieve his *stress*. I know he said he needed to uh, be pent up, but I'm sure—

"Adi." I look up to find Rhys braced over my desk. I was so lost in my little plan I failed to notice him slip through the open doors into my sub-office in the vestibule. That or my six-foot-three boss was hiding behind a pot plant.

"I'm just—"

He puffs out a breath but the tension doesn't leave his shoulders. "There's an event I'd like you to accompany me to this evening."

"In public?" I squeak.

"Yes. The London Maths Syndicate." His face shutters just as my tummy bounces. "Is that a problem?"

We'll be pretending to be a real couple again. We haven't done that since the wedding and... Yeah it might be an issue because how am I going to stop? Who is protecting my heart here? Not me and my clever decisions, that's for sure. And how on earth can I naturally touch this man like I'm truly his wife, allow him to make me come on the sofa when we get home, then go off to my own bed thinking about how all that hardness isn't being... Shall we say utilised?

"No. It's not a problem, Mr Cavendish." A bit of formality. Distance, that's what I need.

"Go out now and buy yourself a new dress and anything else you want. A driver is waiting." He straightens and I catch his brows furrowing as he tosses a card onto my desk, then turns on his heel and stalks to the open entrance to his office. "Be ready at five. *Mrs Cavendish*."

Is that a taunt? I pull it towards me and examine the face. It's a platinum credit card. And the name?

Mrs Adrianne Cavendish.
That's *me*.

Rhys' blue eyes light up when he catches sight of me as I walk into the private ballroom of a hotel so swanky I don't even know its name, but all the staff know mine. It's intimidating and I feel like a girl playing dress-up as I approach the group of older men—all outstandingly handsome but Rhys with his dark hair and height is instantly recognisable to my eyes, like my body knows him. Dressed in a black dinner jacket, he's gorgeous like saw-him-in-a-movie stunning. That jawline. Ooof. I'm not a girl in a dress, I'm a bag of hormones corralled into silk screaming for that testosterone-filled man.

He steps away from the knot of a dozen or so well-dressed people he's talking with, and takes in my deep emerald-green dress approvingly.

I chose it with a lot of encouragement from the personal shopper who met me at the door of the exclusive Oxford Street store. The four bodyguards who followed me around added to the sense of unreality. I wouldn't usually pick something so showy, but she insisted it made my eyes appear even greener, that she had strict instructions to style me to the highest level, and that I looked great.

"You look beautiful," he whispers into my ear as he pulls me in for a soft kiss on the cheek. "This was a perfect choice, my good girl."

I melt.

How does this man not use praise at the office? He could save on staffing bills because all the women would work for free if he just said they were a good girl. They would until I stopped it. Because I'm so jealous. I'd elbow anyone that he called *his* good girl out the window. I want to be his only one.

He smells like warmth and man and fresh air, and I breathe him in as he holds me for a second longer than a casual greeting.

Then he doesn't let me go as he whispers, "Ready?"

I nod, even though I don't think I am. Rhys keeps hold of me as we approach the group, who all look up. They're mainly couples, and I notice that their age gaps are pretty hefty, similar to mine and Rhys'. The women are all dressed up and regarding me with friendly interest. The men are scowling at each other and you can tell they're on their best behaviour, but all are armed for warfare. Like they've got more serious concerns than mathematics. Their gazes slide right over me to Rhys, like they recognise he's a lion who might attack if he thinks they're interested in his lioness.

There's a pause in the talk.

"This is my wife. Adrianne Cavendish."

My tummy does a rolling flutter, but violent. The possessive way Rhys says his wife makes me a butterfly caught in a hairdryer.

"Adi, these are the London *Maths* Syndicate."

A couple of mouths twitch, and one man looks away and coughs.

Hmmm. *Maths*. Sure. Even I recognise some of these men from the gossip magazines. The mafia boss of Westminster is notorious, seen in all the right places being charitable and exerting influence.

"I'm pleased to meet you all." I pretend not to notice they're all pretending for the sake of my husband. It's rude to point it out, and the last thing I want is for anyone to call me on my faking with Rhys. "Can't wait to hear about your mathematical studies."

A blonde woman hides her smile as she steps forward and shakes my hand. "I'm Jessa Lambeth. Let's leave these growly bears to their *calculations* until dinner."

"Sure." I go to move towards her, and I swear that Rhys' fingers tighten on my waist before he releases me.

7

RHYS

Three weeks since I married my secretary, I don't care that I'm a cliche, because I think there's progress. Adi is getting increasingly impatient with the rhythm we've settled into. Breakfast together. Working together. Lunch and stolen kisses in the office. Then the best bit of the day: taking my wife home, laying her down, and using my mouth and fingers to make her come.

Every day is made up of seventy to eighty hours, I swear. That's how long it feels, even if I drag Adi out of the office at three.

Today, I can't leave early. There's a meeting of my senior team presenting ideas for increasing profitability. I called this meeting, and even chose the time so I could ask Adi to take notes and let it drag on a bit so I'd have a reason for her to stay late with me. Now she's sitting across the desk as she always does, tablet in hand, typing up notes and looking like temptation in a neat black shift dress that hugs her curves. Her toffee and cream hair is piled up on her head. I've never seen it down. Bloody stupid. I've kissed her, I've made her come, but I haven't got the guts to confess how much I want to see all that satin flowing over her shoulders or wrapped around my fist.

I try to concentrate on the meeting, and making it end sooner. I should have insisted we reschedule, despite Adi's protest that everyone had now rearranged their schedule to suit me, and it was being a bosshole to alter it at the last minute.

"No." "Fine." "Change the font but then it's fine." I'm being more abrupt than usual, and Adi is glaring at me. I don't stop. "No." "No." "Don't show that to me again." I'm impatiently rejecting any idea that would require discussion.

From the corner of my eye, I notice Adi moving. I really have to get her out of here, not be distracted by my beautiful wife.

I'm determinedly watching the computer screen when there's a touch to my ankle.

What?

Just as I'm about to swat away the—I look down to find Adi kneeling at my feet, beneath my desk, looking up at me with a sly smile.

Video meetings are not sexy. They're not. But the sight of her on her knees makes my cock instantly stiff.

"The long-term profitability..." The sound of the presentation from the Edinburgh branch fades into the background as Adi runs her hand up my leg. She rests her cheek on my inner thigh, and through the fine fabric her heat is a brand.

"Boss. Boss?"

There's a cough and I realise I've been staring at my lap when usually I pay close attention in these meetings. I'm known for being demanding.

"Yes," I snap, looking back at the screen. "Carry on."

And as the man continues the presentation, Adi takes me at my word too.

I stare fixedly as, with tentative movements, she undoes my belt and releases my cock. She lets out a tiny gasp as she encircles it with her hand and it requires all my strength not to allow any sign of what she's doing to show on my face.

Gently, she strokes over the head. It's throbbing. I grip the arms of my chair with white knuckles.

I'm going to hell for this. Because she isn't doing this as my fake wife, or for me to breed her. And god help me, but I want to know what she'll do. Getting onto your knees for your boss—oh fuck just those words in my mind enhance the slow way she's touching me—isn't something you do on a Friday afternoon at work without consideration. We haven't discussed what else she hasn't done, beyond her being a virgin, but I find myself hoping this is a first for her too, as it is for me.

She moves at her own pace, and I let her. Her touch is cautious, like she might hurt me, but I'm a statue. If I acknowledge this, I'll have to stop it.

Her breath over the swollen head of my cock causes a sizzle of pleasure down my spine all the way to my balls, which contract and a drop of precome escapes. My brain is putty as the warmth of her breath is replaced by the smallest contact—her tongue. She laps up that precome and I harden further.

That seems to embolden her. I choke as she pops her hot wet mouth over the helmet and sucks like I'm her favourite lollipop. A cough covers how affected I am, and I feel more than hear her chuckle. Vixen. Siren.

So when I bring my hand down from where I covered my mouth, although it should return to where I was holding the chair arm, it doesn't. Of its own accord, it goes to my lap, and behind Adi's head.

Two can play the game of, surprise! But instead of pulling her head onto my cock so it hits the back of her throat, I grope around blindly for whatever is tying up her hair. She hums and bobs her mouth over me, her hand encircling the rest of my shaft—most of it anyway. Small hands and big dick ought not to be a perfect combination, but the fact she can't cover it all turns me on even more. I find a pin and pull it out as someone on screen gives a very animated presentation on some brightly-coloured pie charts that are all blurry to me.

For every pin I remove, my movements subtle so no one will know, she takes more of me in retaliation, pushing my cock further, sucking me harder. I'm shaking as I comb my fingers through her hair, all tumbled down now.

And yet I still haven't looked. I'm relying entirely on my imagination for how that blonde hair is falling over her cheek. There's only a slight tickle as it slides over my balls. She's everything soft and sexy. Her mouth, her hand that is pumping my shaft, her hair. It's too good and I have to see her taking my cock and her hair undone.

The temptation is beyond anything I'm strong enough to resist.

I flick my gaze down for the briefest moment. Adi is looking right up into my face, those green eyes full of challenge. Mouth slick and pinkened from rubbing over me, her hands on my cock and easing over my thigh. And her hair is more amazing than I thought possible. It's a cascade of honey blonde in all shades that reaches right over her breasts and further in waves.

I can't control this. She's going to make me blow and there will be nothing I can do to stop it. Her mouth, fuck, the feeling of her mouth over my cock. And I can't see anything except the image, tattooed on my eyeballs, from when I glanced down.

"Pause the meeting." I've turned off the microphone and camera before I finish the words and turn and meet Adi's pale green eyes staring up at me, smiling, her lips around *my cock*.

"Minx. What do you think you're doing?" I push my fingers further into her hair. She moans and the vibration feels so good, only deep breathing stops me from coming right there, down her throat.

"I'm your assistant." Her voice is muffled. "I'm just trying to assist you with the problem you have."

"You are my wife," I snarl, possessive as if she really were mine. Adi blinks, surprised, and I try to blank my expression. But I don't let go of her hair.

"You won't get pregnant if I come there." It takes every bit of my self-discipline, honed over forty-one years, to drag her head gently away from me.

"But I want to make you come," she whines.

"My rules, not your whims."

"It would work perfectly—"

One sweep of my arm and the pile of papers go crashing to the floor.

"What?"

I truly don't know what I'm going to do as I lean down and pull her up. She squeaks as I sit her on my desk.

My face must be thunder, as she doesn't protest as I arrange her, pushing her thighs open. My heart hammers as I see her white cotton knickers. You'd think I'd have gotten used to how arousing the little innocent underwear she has is. But no.

Am I going to take her here, on a solid wood desk at

work? Really? I'm ready. She says she wants me to come. I need this...

But I want her to be pregnant, and in love with me, way more. And that means no selfish fucking her for the first time as a quicky in the office. I said I wouldn't come until I could put a baby in her, and I bloody well meant it.

Doesn't mean I can't get revenge though.

Checking the camera, I ensure she's completely out of sight. Then I arrange myself in the chair, arms spread out, seemingly relaxed.

Just out of shot, I cup her pussy.

Ideal.

"This is mine." I press the heel of my hand onto her mons. "And you will be a good girl for me."

Whatever else happens, she's my wife, she'll have my child. That's enough ownership for me, and I'll damn well take what I'm entitled to. Including making her come when I say so, and not giving in to any scheme she has to scupper my plan to knock her up.

She nods, eyes wide and a savage beast in my chest gives a roar of satisfaction.

"Now, can you be a good quiet girl while I finish this meeting?"

I school my features into a carefully neutral expression as I look at the computer monitor, unmute, and turn the video back on.

"Shall we continue?"

The meeting progresses and I finger my wife.

I'm not listening, or seeing the faces of my colleagues. Nope. All my attention is on the movement of my fingers between Adi's legs. The feel of her soft, swollen parts. Those pink folds.

She's almost silent. Almost. But she's shifting and

pulsing beneath my touch. That little nub is swelling and getting harder and it's tempting to keep at it hard. I could push her into a quick orgasm.

Or I could torment her for longer, as she meant to do to me. Minx. She vibrates with frustration as my fingers slip from her clit, downwards to her entrance. And though I've had my fingers in her before, it's like the first time all over again as I press into that snug wet passage. Hot, too. She feels amazing.

I'm pretending I'm doing this to punish her, and I'm more interested in the meeting. Keeping my expression totally impassive, I ensure my girl is out of shot but dangerously close to revealing everything. Or so she thinks.

My gaze is trained on the corner of the screen where if she shifted too far she'd appear in the video, and my ears are listening for anything. My mouse is hovered over the mute and off buttons. She wants to play with fire? Absolutely. But I'm here with a bucket of water, because only I get to see and hear Adi come.

"Yes, do it," I reply when I'm asked about an idea for a new advert.

It's not for them, that reply. It's for Adi, and she knows it. Her clit throbs in response.

I'm far more positive than usual, and I can see several rectangles of baffled expressions on screen. I think I agree to proceed with a couple of projects because I'm too distracted by the feel of Adi's soft pussy to say anything but yes. I rock my thumb over her clit as I stroke two fingers into her passage the way I know she likes it. I want to get her off, hard. Something she'll remember. She's so tight and wet, and knowing I did that to her makes my dick just as hard as her mouth on me.

Then there's her gaze. I can feel it burning into my temple.

It sounds implausible, but despite my having had my face between her legs every night, this is just as intimate. Not looking at her, not hearing any of her usual moans and whimpers, and barely touching has forced me to take the smallest of cues. It's testing the limit of our connection, and finding that it's stronger than I realised.

She's nearly there. Her thigh shakes against my forearm.

Good girl. I think the words, but it's like we're so linked, she heard. Because at that moment, she crests. She trembles and pants. Not the uncontrolled cries of pleasure when we're comfortable at home, no. She's my good quiet girl, coming almost silently.

The meeting concludes in five more minutes, during which I keep my fingers in her pussy, holding her.

I thank my staff and click off the video and sound, before turning to Adi. She presses her lips together, cheeks pink.

A final squeeze of that sensitive part of her, and I slide my fingers out, glistening with her arousal. Raising them to my mouth, I cram them in. I suck her sweet and salty cream from my fingers, licking them clean as she watches, entranced.

"I'm addicted to your taste, little one," I rumble.

"I want to make you come," she whispers rebelliously. "It's only fair."

"You will. I'm going to come inside you, deep inside you, here." I brush her abdomen with my wet knuckles. "I'll give you that baby you want."

She lets out a sound like an angry mouse. "I don't..."

Her huff and that glance away intrigues me.

"But for being such a needy girl, there are consequences."

Her breath hitches.

I do not ask about what that, *I don't*, meant. Because what if it's that she's changed her mind and doesn't want a baby anymore? What would we be left with then?

A sham of a marriage and nothing to tie her to me.

Nothing.

Except, perhaps, the drugging pleasure.

"From now on, I'm going to make you come twice a day."

8

ADI

Hormones, huh? They're a trip. I've been tracking my temperature so I know when I'm ovulating, and gotta admit, I'm desperate. Why won't it change? Why is my cycle so looooooonnnnnnggggg?

It's been two weeks since my period, four since I last ovulated, and almost exactly a month since baster-gate, as I'm calling it, and the day Rhys and I got married.

I'm so horny.

Everything reminds me of sex. When Rhys puts a cappuccino on the table at my elbow, I think about how the white froth on the top might look like... Yeah. References to milk make me wild. Any cylindrical object makes my pussy throb. Even a can of fizzy pop. I had to stop and breathe when I saw a cucumber on the salad last night. Dessert was a nightmare. Cherries make me blush. *Bananas?* Get out of here. I can't. Too much.

And guess what drives me most insane?

Rhys. I watch him whenever I can. I have catalogued every part of his body not covered by his suit in obscene, stalker-like detail. That man. I thought he was gorgeous before, when I hadn't felt his hands on me or been shaken to the core—or from the core, rather—by him. Now, it's a whole new level. It's like I've been on a wine—Rhys—tasting course, and suddenly I can recognise and appreciate all the fancy bits about him.

I always fancied my hot boss, as anyone with a pulse would. But now I crave him.

He's oblivious. Or amused. I can't even tell anymore through the fog of twenty-four-hour arousal. The other day I almost let him know, a slip of the tongue. *I don't just want a baby. I want you.*

Thankfully I caught it in time, but doubt scratches at me. What if I get pregnant and he doesn't want me afterwards? What if I don't get pregnant and that makes our whole agreement void? So I refuse to think beyond the baby-making. I take my temperature every day in the morning and pray it shows I'm fertile, so I can *please* have sex with Rhys. And in the evening, just to be sure.

I don't take the thermometer to work with me to try again at lunchtime.

Alright, alright, I do. But I only check about once an hour.

It's just, I'm frantic. I'm hooked on him and he's inflexible. Unyielding. Hard.

Definitely that last one.

He's made me scream with his tongue and fingers every night and morning for a month, and I'm fed up. Not of coming, but of him *not* coming. I don't understand how he isn't frustrated? I'm boiling with impatience on his behalf. Maybe I stole all his sexual frustration, or he gave it to me along with the pleasure. All I know is I need to see that granite hard, silken smooth, heated length of his again, and I really, *really* want it inside me.

So when I take my temperature in the morning, I'm willing it to be higher. Please, please, just a bit higher. It isn't going to be... Then I stare at the numbers on the little digital screen.

I'm fertile.

It's really happening. I'm ready to be bred.

The avalanche of happiness overcomes any fear that this will be the end of him touching me. I really adore the org—him. I adore him.

No, it's... More than that. It's love.

I'm in love with my probably-mafia-boss pretend husband billionaire boss.

Now I admit it in the secrecy of my mind, I can see I've loved him for ages. Maybe even before we met, as I swooned over the photos of him in magazines. He's gorgeous and grumpy and exacting and I wouldn't have him any other way. Except, perhaps, loving.

It's alright, it doesn't matter. I'll cope without the orgasms because I'll have Rhys as the father of my child and my husband for two glorious years.

I'll have his baby and my grandma's great-grandchild.

Throwing myself out of bed, I rush out of my room and across the corridor. I've never been into his bedroom, he's never suggested it. He's licked my pussy in almost every other room of this apartment, and every piece of furniture. But it's like he thinks that if we're in his bed, he won't be able to control himself. Or maybe that I could seduce him into breaking his promise not to come until it's inside me.

But I barge open the door with no warning.

"Rhys!" I'm grinning like it's Christmas. Which it is. It absolutely is.

"Adi." He looks up, shocked and then pleased as I walk into his bedroom. It's painted a deep, soothing blue, with dark wood furniture. The bed is crisp white linen. He's wearing his usual navy suit, and his hands are at his throat, cupping a silk tie.

"I'm fertile!" I wave the thermometer like it's a golden ticket.

He freezes, the smile in place.

"That's..." Coughing, he stares at my pyjamas, gaze flicking down to my bare legs before he closes his eyes for a second like I'm too bright to look at. "Great. Really great."

"Husband." I summon my inner strumpet and walk over to him with a sway in my hips. I'm wearing little pyjama shorts and a high-collared blue and white frilled top, but I pretend I'm an underwear model. He watches every step of the way, a tortured expression creeping over his face. "Please breed me. Fuck a baby into me."

I reach him and—who is this bold woman, she's not me—grasp his tie, using it to pull him down to me as I boost onto tiptoes.

"Adi, we need to talk—" He groans as our mouths touch. He tastes like mint toothpaste and smells of spicy cologne.

When he crushes me to him and kisses me back, I know I've won. It's ravenous, this kiss. The man I love is holding my head and plundering my mouth.

At my belly his erection is a hard hot length, and I'm going to faint with joy. Who cares about the future? I can have that glorious cock inside me. I'll figure tomorrow out—

The kiss stops.

Panic drains all the sexy triumph from me as Rhys puts me from him, stepping backwards, though not relinquishing the hold on my waist.

"I've been thinking," he says seriously, face grave. He looks like he does when he's reading a quarterly financial report and there's an error. Bleak as a rainy Bank Holiday.

I'm not going to like this, am I?

His fingers tighten until it's almost painful. "A baby should have two parents who love each other."

"What?" My heart drops to my ankles and I sway. He sounds so reasonable. I want to argue with him, but what can I retort? That children don't need two loving parents? That's obviously a good thing.

"You don't want to have a baby with me because you don't love me," I say miserably. "Were you ever going to? You promised, Rhys!" I find that much indignation, at least.

"I did promise," he says calmly.

"Was all this a lie?" I wrench from his grasp, hurting, sore. I'm betrayed and angry and so, so… I think I'm going to cry.

"No. Adi, stop it and listen to me." He brings his hands to my shoulders and hesitates, grip tightening. "I want to have a baby with you. I want you to be my wife for real."

My heart hammers against my ribs. I'm dreaming. The pain melts away.

"I'm asking," he continues, and his chest expands as he drags in a breath. "Do you think you could love me? Maybe? One day?"

One day? Is he kidding?

"You want me to love you?"

"Yes." And in that one word there is more stripped bare, vulnerable honesty than I ever thought I'd have from Rhys. His Adam's apple bobs as he swallows and I have the oddest compulsion to stroke his neck and soothe that fear away.

"I do love you."

The shock is almost comical. My grumpy boss is speechless, mouth open, blinking. Then I'm in his arms, being crushed to his chest as he kisses me so hard I think he might break his nose. Or our teeth. Clothes are yanked off in his hurry. I had no idea a man could multitask, but apparently Rhys can kiss me, hold me, and strip off his shirt and mine, simultaneously. Admittedly, I'm not wearing much, and I'm helping. I wriggle out of my pyjama bottoms and hold my arms up for him to pull the top off. And somehow he rids himself of everything, so when I'm naked, it's his skin on mine that takes up all my attention, not how we've never been like this. There's an unleashed, feral edge to Rhys. He's been so controlled as he makes me come and takes nothing for himself, and that restraint is cracking.

Until he stiffens.

"Wait-wait-wait." Hauling me to the bed, he sits us both on the edge.

I let out a frustrated laugh-sob, since he was the one tearing off clothes. But this pause gives me the opportunity to look at him, finally. He's just in his boxers and I'm utterly distracted by the view of his sculpted chest, covered with scars and a smattering of dark hair over his pectorals then in a happy trail that leads enticingly down to where the fabric and that impressive bulge starts. I've had that mammoth length in my mouth, and need him everywhere. I want to bite him. Consume him. He's so beautiful, the scars only enhancing his raw appeal.

"Later," I murmur as I reach for his cock. He grunts, but covers my hand with his.

"No more misunderstandings between us." He laces his fingers with mine and shifts my touch from his cock.

We both look down to our joined hands. He's so much bigger than me and excitement tumbles through my stomach.

"You know that I love you."

I did not know this, and though I suppose it was

inferred, hearing Rhys say so makes my heart expand to almost painfully squash into my ribcage.

"I have a confession."

Oh no. No, please...

"You should know, before..." He winces, heaves in a breath, and sighs. "I have to tell you about my work. Not all of my business is entirely legal."

"You're a mafia boss."

"You knew?" The thread of uncertainty in his tone is endearing.

It's sweet how he thinks he kept it hidden from me. "Your friends are not very interested in maths, given how much of your accounting doesn't add up."

"My clever girl," he replies softly, face unscrunching. "You don't mind?"

"Not that. I minded when you wouldn't make me yours. When you denied me," I reveal in a whisper.

"I could never resist you." He tugs my hand gently and brings it to his lips, kissing my knuckles. "You're so beautiful you have your own orbit."

Obviously I'm not. But he makes me feel I might be as he trails reverent kisses over my wrist and up my arm.

"You caught me in it the second we met, Adi. I was yours from that moment onwards."

I feel like a goddess. A giant. I am more powerful than a lightning bolt and more beautiful than a sunset. Then I'm flat on my back with Rhys over me, and there's nothing between us. Awareness sparks through me. The yielding, cool softness of the bed, and the hot smoothness of Rhys' skin as he covers me. He's a massive, dark, hungry predator with his prey in sight. And I'm his happy sacrificial rabbit. His heavy erection snags on my inner thigh. I wriggle and shift until... Oh yes. We both groan as his hardness notches at my entrance. I spread my legs shamelessly, and rock against him.

"You're so wet for me." Holding himself on his elbows, he looks into my eyes and strokes my cheeks with infinite care. "I'm going to fuck you so hard and thoroughly you'll be feeling the echoes for a week," he says with deceptive gentleness as he puts a little more pressure onto my folds. "I have to have you."

"Take me," I beg. And it's true. I need him. I'm crazy for this man.

The press of his cock into my soaked pussy is heaven, and I roll my hips as he eases down and—pop. He's inside me. Just the tip, but he's so big, it stretches me. Every part of me is vibrating. I'm more alive than I've ever been. It's like there's electricity generated by Rhys and me being together.

"You're mine." He slips another inch. "Feel that? It's me claiming your body the way you've claimed my heart, Adi."

I can't reply. I'm too busy focusing on where he's spearing into me, opening me up.

"Say it, Adi."

"Yes." I reply through the fog.

"The words."

I try to think past the mixture of pleasure and pain. The sensation of fullness is so alien and yet achingly familiar, like we've been doing this in previous lives. In a way, we have. He's had his fingers in me every night for a month. I'm intimately acquainted with the swirl of stubble on his jawline and his weight on me. This is just one step further. I'm a freaking feminist. Virginity doesn't mean anything, it's a patriarchal concept I don't even subscribe to.

All those rationalisations don't alter the fact that this feels more special than when we exchanged vows. That was both of us with layers of fake and real. This is passionate and breath stealing. This is so intimate, I think I'll never be the same again.

Rhys *taking* my virginity, and *giving* me his baby?

Oof. So hot.

I clutch at him to bring him closer and he slips another inch deeper and I'm losing my mind.

This is just us, nothing else. Simply the magic of two people meant to be together.

"Adi, say it," he growls. And it's a good thing he reminds me because he's splitting me open in the best way and it leaves little room for carrying on a cohesive dialogue. "Say you belong to me, wife."

A thrill zips up my spine at the way he calls me wife. He's said it before, but not with that meaning. His *wife*.

"I'm yours, husband." The confession is ripped from me.

He groans with satisfaction and I'm rewarded with another inch then a pull and push, sending shivers of pleasure flying from everywhere we're joined.

"Yes, that's it." He kisses me tenderly. "I love you so much, sweetheart. You're mine, and I'm having you."

I make a noise like an animal as he's deeper again, slipping further and I swear it takes both of us by surprise when he bottoms out, as far in as possible.

"Tell me all this cream is just for me." He lifts up and thrusts, and I'm overwhelmed.

"It is, it is," I plead.

"Tell me how you want my cock. How you love it." His voice is gravelly.

"I do. I love the feel of your cock. More. Please."

"Fuck, you're so wet, you make it impossible to hold back," he whispers as he begins to move in a rolling rhythm that doesn't stop, keeping up the slick friction. "Nothing has ever felt as good as your soaking pussy taking my cock. You were meant for me."

I bob my head rapidly in agreement. He's so hot and smooth and hard, I think he was made for me too. The feeling of where we're joined is pure magic.

"Adi, look."

I'm confused for a second because his head is bowed and he's holding himself off me, muscles taut, his gaze between our bodies at where his cock is disappearing into me in a rhythmic pattern. Excitement zings from my clit right to my toes and I stare.

"Put your hand here." He doesn't wait, grabbing my wrist and pressing my palm to the lowest part of my abdomen. "Feel that. Feel how I'm inside you all the way."

He thrusts into me deep and slow, and oh god. Yes. I can feel that. And again. Every thrust he's rearranging my insides, very literally. My tummy presses into my hand as he fills me. That is his cock, pushing up into me.

I have no idea why this is so hot, but it's like I can touch him through my body. I shove my hand down onto my own skin and he groans.

"Adi, I'll come too fast if you do that."

It's making me even tighter around him, and surely that's good? "But you said you were going to fill me up."

"Oh I will." He lifts his head and grins, blue eyes twinkling. "Don't worry about that. The trouble you'll have now I've started is stopping me filling you, every hour of every day, from now until eternity."

9

RHYS

Even though I know we have a lifetime to find out everything about each other, I need our first time to be embedded in her memory as it will be in mine. That means the joy of experimenting to find the ways we fit together best. Adi writhes and pants and moans as I intersperse shallow pumps with deep pounding thrusts. I tease the head of my cock with the tightness of her entrance then press all the way, right to her limit. I watch her face ravenously. I'm compelled.

What I want more than anything is for her to need this as badly as I do, again and again and again.

I think I'm succeeding. However, she hasn't come yet, and call me superstitious, but I am absolutely serious about her coming so she'll get pregnant.

We're chest to chest, and our kisses are sloppy, and although I adore having her trapped beneath me, I've got other plans too.

I push her legs out, wider, more exposed. It alters the angle, making her gasp.

"More of that, huh?" No disagreement from me. She

came so damn quick the other day I was almost disappointed when I held her thighs wide open and spread her pussy out. Being inside her when she's like this is mind-blowing.

"You feel so good, sweetheart. I love that there's nothing between us. No condom. No birth control. It's just you and me, bare."

"Yes." She clutches at the back of my head. "Husband."

I need more of her. Without stopping driving into her, holding her hips I sit on my heels and pull her onto my lap. In the same moment, I push hard.

We both moan at the deeper penetration. She's laid before me clutching the bedsheets, and I can see every part of her beautiful body, including my cock being swallowed by her pink wet slit.

Easing out, I drive in again, then settle into a rhythm as her eyes flutter shut. "I'm going to fuck a baby into you. Our baby, sweetheart. I love you so much."

Holding her tight by one hip, I bring my fingers to her clit. It barely takes more than a touch for her to respond. She tightens around my cock as I rub circles over that sensitive nub, watching her face.

The desire to breed her is making my balls tingle.

"You remember what we said about you coming?" I gasp out. "About it helping get you pregnant?"

"Yes? No?" She thrashes her head from side to side, losing it. Mindless with the pleasure. I don't know if the "no" is an acknowledgement of the fact I was speaking absolute nonsense, or denial that she ever heard my paper-thin excuse for making her come every night and morning.

"I need to feel you clenching around my cock again, sweetheart. I have to feel you come before I do."

And that is true. Because I want this to be as perfect for

her as it is for me. I crave seeing that pleasure on her face again.

"Now be a good girl for me." I press harder on her clit and circle over it faster as I adjust the angle of my length inside her again. "And come."

I don't know if it was the command or the touch, maybe both, but she grips around me and cries out. I'm familiar with the sounds and sight of her climax after a whole month, though I love seeing it more every time I do this for her. But feeling her come on my cock? Next level.

"You're so fucking gorgeous when you come," I tell her, but I don't think she hears. I can barely hear anything myself for the rush of blood in my ears and the desperate desire to follow her over into orgasm. But I also don't want to miss any part of her coming on my cock this first time. So I watch her writhe, slowly pumping into her, relishing the feel of her soaked pussy. She's creamed all over me.

Her heated silk tight around my cock and nothing could possibly feel as good, except perhaps seeing the pleasure on her face from only inches away.

I need to kiss her. I lean forwards and lick her breasts on the way up, shifting over her, getting a bit distracted by her sweet nipples. But eventually I have her beneath me again, pinned by my cock and trapped by my arms either side of her head.

She's ruined, eyes half closed, mouth open. I kiss her lips and cheeks as my thrusts accelerate again.

"I'm going to come inside you, hot and deep," I whisper into her ear. "I'm going to make you overflow with seed. Then I'll make you hold it in, even while it's too much, while it drips out of you. I'm going to keep every drop to make you pregnant."

I didn't know I had a breeding kink, but apparently I do, as the shit I'm saying as I fuck my girl is absolutely filthy.

Then because I can, and maybe because I can't help it, I tangle my fingers into the acres of wavy blonde hair haloed around her head, loose from when she slept with it unbound. It's silk. Everything about Adi is soft and perfect.

Then I tug. Her head tilts back and her eyes fly open at the hint of pain. She whines and her passage flutters tighter.

I do it again, wrapping a handful around my fist and tugging a bit harder. She gasps my name this time. For all I dreamed of holding that blonde hair, reality is even better. Her hair in my fingers forces her to reveal her throat and I kiss her there, along with possessive bites that make her hips roll with mine.

"What did I do to deserve you?" I murmur.

I can't get near enough. I need to be everywhere. If I could, I'd consume her, or be swallowed whole by her.

"I love you so much. You're my obsession, my everything, my dream. It's a good thing you agreed to our marriage, because I would never have allowed you to go, sweetheart."

"I'll never leave you. I've got you now." She punctuates that statement with a squeeze of her pelvic floor muscles, gripping me.

"I cannot live without you. I love you. Say you love me."

"Rhys."

"Say it," I insist. I'm probably fucking her too hard, but she seems to like it.

But what I want more than to possess her is for her to have to stay because she's addicted to me and the way I make her feel. I want her to feel the same desperation I do.

I guess she does, since she's holding me as tightly as I am her.

"I'm yours."

Something unravels in my back and I mash our lips together in an attempt to be more closely joined with her. A tension I didn't realise I was carrying, even after we'd confessed our love for each other. That she's mine feeds a primal need inside me. Maybe I'll always lust after claiming her.

"I have to pound you into the mattress, wife." I let up on our kiss to plead. "Tell me that's what you want too."

"Yes. Harder. Deeper," she encourages me, shifting around beneath me and clutching at my lower back as she tries to get what she desires. "Breed me."

Oh definitely.

Reaching down, I cram my hand between us, but not letting up my thrusts. "Come again and I'll give you everything I have. A whole month's worth of seed just for you, sweetheart. Right up against your womb."

My good, responsive girl hardly requires anything extra. She comes, digging her fingers into my back hard enough to leave marks. I hope they do. I'm certainly going to give her something to remember this morning.

I ride out her orgasm by pressing my mouth to hers and not watching this one, just experiencing her tight wet heat and continuing to pound into her.

"Rhys," she pants. "Fill me up." She reaches up and scrapes her nails firmly over my scalp. I open my eyes and it's only then I realise she's recovered from the pinnacle I threw her off. Bright and thoroughly fucked, her eyes are hooded by determination.

"Come inside me, Rhys. I want to see you break apart for me."

My hips keep pistoning into her and I'm drowning in her pale green eyes. Tropical-beach-water eyes.

"Your love, your seed, a baby." A little smirk, and for half a second I wonder what that's about. Then I feel her clench around me. Holding the sensitive head of my cock in a vice-like grip. "Give it to me."

Pleasure triggers. I can't get out words to dirty talk or prepare her.

Orgasm shudders down my back in white hot sparks. I shake. It's so strong, so good it's painful. It's way too much even as I know I'll want this again every day of my life.

But I don't close my eyes. Neither does Adi. She watches me greedily, as hungry for my orgasm as I am. Probably more. She strokes my hair with affectionate softness as she grips my cock, feeling like she's milking out every drop.

My muscles give out as I empty myself into her. Not just my balls. My heart. My soul. I'm ruined over this woman. I'd give her everything then break down myself to atoms and offer her those too, to wear as a crown.

I collapse, wracked with the emotion of finally coming in Adi. Of breeding my girl. Every spurt is accompanied by pleasure so intense my brain is jelly. I've got no thoughts, just love and devotion and yearning for my *wife*.

EPILOGUE
RHYS

6 years later

I wake to the warmth of my wife's body curled into my chest, and a wash of contentment rises in me. I run a hand down her side, pausing at her thigh. So soft. I love how she has become a bit more curved after six years and two children.

My cock hardens as I explore her curves, the rise and fall of her breath slow and relaxed while I map her skin. Again. No day passes without me touching every part of my wife.

Fuck. My wife. My cock is rock-solid now, nestled against her peachy arse.

I kiss her neck and shift down. I wonder if...

"Daddy!"

Uuugfh.

Baby blocked. What an irony.

I look up to find Poppy peeking in through the bedroom door. I adore that our eldest child is capable, brave, and inquisitive like her mother. But sometimes would it hurt for her to stay in bed after six? I think not. Her little brother manages it, although at only two years old, Mark is different. Quieter and gentler than his sister. If anyone is going to take over the Canary Wharf mafia, it will be Poppy.

"Good morning, little one."

"Can I come in?" She scuffs her bare feet on the threshold.

We had to implement clear rules for the kids about not coming into our bedroom and jumping onto the bed after one particularly close call last year when we forgot to lock the door. Yeah. Baby making is fun, but not with babies watching.

"We're going to let Mummy sleep," I tell her in a whisper. "Quiet voices."

Poppy creases her brow in confusion. "But it's her birthday."

Well, Daddy was trying to give her a special birthday present when you arrived in the room. I don't say that. "She does, but she'd like to sleep a bit longer while we make breakfast and check her presents are ready."

"Presents?" Poppy is immediately interested. She loves gifts, both giving and receiving.

"Can you put your dressing gown on and I'll see you downstairs?"

Poppy nods happily and skips away and I look wistfully after her. She was conceived the first time Adi and I made love, surprising her but not me when we found out. I pointed out that we barely got out of bed for the first week of our proper marriage. She let me have her so many times a day in the end I had to insist we took a break because I couldn't bear to see her wince as she walked. I mean, never walking anywhere again and leaving her tied to the bed did go through my mind as an option, but I managed to do the right thing and enforce rehydration and non-sexual activities for twelve hours before I mauled her back into bed and she rode me gleefully.

I take a moment to look at Adi. Ridiculously gorgeous. Twenty-nine today and she's just as beautiful as the day I met her. More so, actually.

Adi stirs a little as I nuzzle her jawline. "Mmm. Is it time to get up?"

"Hello birthday girl. Not yet. Stay in bed," I whisper into her ear. "I'll make pancakes."

She makes a contented hum and snuggles deeper into the covers.

I really, really want to stay with my wife, but the idea of a five-year-old alone in the kitchen is strong motivation. I get up, only leaving one more kiss on her forehead before throwing on clothes and heading to Mark's room. Our two-year-old is contentedly sitting in his crib playing with soft rabbits.

"Hey champ."

He looks up with a bright smile and waves his rabbit at me. It's a bit sticky where he's been mouthing it. Or cuddling? Who knows. I lift him up, do a quick check, and carry him downstairs.

When both kids are safely ensconced in their chairs and drinking milk, I whip up pancake mixture.

"Flip it!" demands Poppy as I begin to cook the first one.

And because my kids are my whole life, I get a second frying pan and flip the first pancake for them, over and over again to their shrieks and giggles, until the next pancake is cooked. To think I used to spend my time working, murdering my enemies, and working some more.

Now we've taken the business that Adi worked at legit—and she's the joint CEO—we make as much money but without the risk of being attacked by another London mafia. And I know it sounds indulgent, but my family comes first now, above work.

"What's Mummy's extra present?" Poppy asks as she stuffs her face with pancake.

I take the wrapped box containing Adi's family-friendly present from the shelf, and show it to my daughter, whose eyes go wide at the fancy wrapping paper and satin bow.

"Ooo. Can I see what's inside?" says Poppy, and Mark makes grabby hands.

I chuckle. Insatiably curious, both our kids. This is why the sexy gifts remain in our bedroom. Adi will see it when she wakes up, and hopefully I'll see it on her this evening. "You'll see when Mummy opens it later when we see Great-grandma."

Poppy's little face creases with conflicted emotions. The children love to see their great-grandmother and she spoils them rotten. They've done a helicopter ride every week to visit her since before they were old enough to walk.

"But Great-granny will have presents for her and toffees for us. Mummy could open this now."

"Mummy could open what?" Adi walks into the kitchen wrapped in a flowing white silk robe that reaches her knees and is tied at the front with a belt. Her blonde hair is all over her shoulders and a shot of desire goes through me, even though our kids are right there and she's just casually come down for breakfast.

There are cries of happy birthday, and demands for birthday kisses and I let it all happen as I serve up pancakes for each of them. Lemon and sugar for Adi—always tart and sweet, my girl, chocolate spread for Poppy, and maple syrup for Mark. I'll have some with peanut butter and strawberries once the rest of my family is stuffed. All served on matcha-tea-green plates.

"Are you going to eat?" Adi asks as I return to cook more pancakes.

We exchange a look above the kids' heads, where I say, *I wouldn't mind eating your pussy* and she says, *I know you love to eat out.*

"Not yet," I reply mildly.

"It's my birthday, and I would like my husband to sit down and have breakfast with us rather than just cook."

I huff with laughter at the way she specified breakfast and not eating. I like to care for my family. Protect them all. I saunter over to Adi and lean down, my hands running down her sides.

"When the kids are in bed tonight I'll do anything you like," I whisper into her ear.

She turns in my arms and gives me a grin so downright wicked I have to hold her because I swear all the blood in my body has rushed to my cock.

"Anything?" she replies, eyes glittering.

"Anything at all." And I wonder what I've gotten myself in for.

EXTENDED EPILOGUE
ADI

6 YEARS LATER, THAT EVENING

There are three things I know for sure. One, this practically see-through designer negligee that Rhys bought me for my birthday is magic, and worth every penny he spent on it. Two, I'm horny. Three, I am in exactly the right place.

"What do you want as a treat, birthday girl?" Rhys asks as he closes the bedroom door behind him and places the baby monitor onto a chest of drawers.

I think it's a hangover from the earliest days of our marriage, but when Rhys asks me what I want, it's always the same answer. "To make you come in my mouth."

He gives me a wry look. "We've talked about this. That is not a luxury for you, sweetheart, that's one for me."

"Nope." I shake my head. "Extra protein. A delicious salty treat. That's what I want for my birthday."

Shaking his head, he approaches with measured steps, taking me in.

"You look fucking delicious in that scrap of lace. I cannot wait to push it aside and see your pussy." He pulls me into his arms, one hand at my lower back and the other tangling in my hair, and although I didn't see a bulge when he entered our bedroom, there's no denying his erection now. It's a hard rod between us.

The kiss is possessive and taking, his tongue thrusting into my mouth. And then he does the thing that really makes me crazy.

"On your knees," he murmurs.

My kingpin. When he's like this, I remember that he's grumpy and a bit scary. Bigger than me. I remember the thrill of nervous excitement when I'd see him in the morning when he was only my boss.

I drop and fumble for his flies, glancing up at him with a grin. Tall. So flipping tall, my lovely husband.

Rhys tsks. "Cushion, Adi."

Ack! I scramble to get something to pillow my knees. Rhys won't allow me even the smallest discomfort, and it's sweet, it really is, but there's carpet on the floor. He's overprotective.

And uncompromising, so I don't argue. I get a cushion, and sink to my knees before him. A slight smile plays around his mouth as he watches me release his belt.

Mmmm. He's heated and rock-solid as I reveal his erection from black boxers and my mouth waters.

I can't wait. I push the fabric down a little further so his balls hang down too. I start there, with a caress that makes him rumble a purr from his throat.

Working my way up, I rub my face over him. I know it's weird, but the silk of his cock on my cheek is the best sensation. The scent of him—musky and masculine—is too delicious. I love him so much, I want to cover myself in him. Sometimes, when I'm a really good girl, I get to be covered in his come.

Today though is a different pleasure. The first lick is heaven. All the way up his length, I kiss and tongue him. I control the pace at this point, teasing us both by not quite getting to where we want him to be: in my throat, taking his pleasure,

He lets out a growl as I cover the rounded crown of his cock with my lips. My tongue swirls over him. He's hot, smooth steel and I can't get enough. He fills my mouth completely. I suck. My cheeks hollow and I use both hands on the part of him I can't get in, stroking up and down, slipping to cup his balls every now again.

"You're so beautiful taking my cock."

"Mmmm." I hum my approval and get into a rhythm. His hands stroke over my neck, then comb up into my hair. His slight tug sensitises me, sending a delicious shiver right down to my core. Combined with the feel of his hardness makes me so slippery between the legs. Hot. Needy. My nipples are begging for attention too. They'll have to wait, as I'm all-in for making my husband crazy with my mouth. But I do indulge in one thing that's another gift.

"Do you love me?" I say around his cock, slipping my lips fully back over his cock as I look up at him and see affection as well as lust in his gaze. And that's why I'm confident in his response.

He loves me. I'm sure. But as I have his cock in my mouth it's my favourite thing to have him say filthy things. I'm addicted to all of my husband, including his declarations of love.

"Yes and no," he replies, a little teasing.

My heart jumps uncomfortably. What does he mean, *no*?

"Love is a normal emotion for normal people." He tightens his grip on my hair, possessive, and a little controlling. My pussy floods with moisture. God but it makes me so hot when he does that.

"I love you, but it's far more than love."

I moan around his cock, trying to get it deeper. Yes. This is what I wanted. My pussy gushes with fresh slickness. I love it when he says things like this.

"I adore you. I'm obsessed."

I bob up and down, keeping my tempo even with his words. His cock is hard and smooth in my mouth. I can't take it all and as it hits the back of my throat it chokes me a bit. Deeper. Harder. I want to take all of him.

"You're my first thought in the morning and my last at night," he says, voice hoarse. "I love our kids in an appropriate way, Adi. But nothing about how I feel about *you* is something I could confess to anyone else. You're the reason I do everything, you have me entirely within your control."

I suck harder and my neck is sore from the pace, but then he takes over.

"But I crave ownership too."

Suddenly, I'm not giving, he's taking. My head is cradled in his big hands and he thrusts into my throat, making me gag and my eyes water. But just as he promised, I feel owned. Body and soul, I belong to this man. I open my throat as best I can—never quite managed the trick, mainly I suspect because Rhys won't let me practise very often.

"You're *mine*, sweetheart." He shakes, thrusting harder, and just as it's too much, as it hurts in the best way because I can feel how good it is for him, he comes. Hot and salty and uniquely him, he fills my mouth with spurt after spurt. I swallow it down, struggling to do so with him still filling me with his come and his cock.

He holds my gaze the whole time, those blue eyes

intense, obsessed. I love that about him. I never have to doubt that Rhys wants me.

Gently, he pulls my head back. His cock pops out with an obscenely wet pop.

He sinks back onto the edge of the bed and pulls me to sit over his lap.

"Fuck, Adi. You destroy me in the best way. I think I just died."

My smile is smug. Really, really smug.

Ha. I love it when I ruin him. Favourite thing.

And I'm still feeling self-satisfied when he flips me over with a rough growl.

"Rhys!"

"What?" He shoves up the negligee, revealing little lace knickers. "You know what happens now, darling."

"No fair," I grumble, even as my pussy pulses with desire.

"That's the rule, Adi." The words come between biting kisses to my nipples.

I know. I let him remove the scrap of lace, helping him with a lift and a wriggle. The rule is simple and the source of some argument between us. I think that I should be able to give him about forty-five-ish orgasms to catch up with the ones he gave me in our first month of marriage.

His rule is that for every time he comes, I come at least once. Usually twice. On some very memorable nights, I've had to beg for mercy. Around six, but I'm not counting at that point.

"I don't like the rule... Ohhh. Yes."

Rhys has kissed down my torso and begins to lick my pussy like it's his passion. Like it's everything and oh it's amazing. I'm already amped up from giving him a blow job and he takes advantage of that, licking me hard, shoving me into pleasure.

It's quick. He holds down my hips and forces it on me.

"Mine," he snarls between sucks to my clit, his fingers pumping into me.

I come instantly. That word. Being *his* sends spirals of white-hot pleasure through me. I see stars. My insides clench and throb.

"See, that wasn't so difficult, was it, my good girl." Rhys' tone is slathered with amusement as my twitches and pulses subside.

He gathers me into his arms. I'm practically unconscious. The echo of him is in my mouth and my clit and my insides where his fingers were. It's the best feeling.

"Adi, you're sublime," he murmurs sleepily. "To think I wasted all that time pining after you when we could have been doing that."

"What would you have done if you'd walked into the office ten minutes later, Rhys?" I don't know why I say it now, but... Well, he's so possessive of me and our kids. I wonder sometimes if this would all never have happened if fate hadn't intervened.

I guess it's fear of how close I was to never having all of this.

I love him. He loves me. It wasn't ruined by me being pregnant by someone else, but maybe some destructive part of my brain thinks it could have been. That I was one mistake away from missing out on the love of my life.

"When?" He props himself up on his forearm and looks at me with indulgent confusion. Awake again. Anything that concerns me, he's on it. He always knows.

"*The* day," I say teasingly. "Turkey baster day."

"The day I proposed to the love of my life, you mean?"

"Yeah, that day. What if you didn't find out until months later? I would have been pregnant with another man's—"

"No, you wouldn't," he cuts me off with the supreme confidence—some would say arrogance, including past me—I adore. "It was always my child."

"But it wouldn't have been your genetic child," I insist. Who knew this was a wound I wanted to open? On my birthday of all days. Why am I doing this?

I guess because I have to know. I've shoved this tiny concern to the back of my mind forever, because it really doesn't matter. It didn't happen.

Rhys sighs and gives me a look that bridges annoyed and patient. "Adi, who did you think about when you were trying to order sperm?"

After six years of marriage, you'd think I couldn't be embarrassed by anything. He saw our kids being born. He's seen me on the loo, and he's rolled his eyes at the way I devour pancakes. But I flush.

"You," I admit.

He nods, a smug smile on his face. "And who do you think I was dreaming about every night when I stroked my cock?"

"Me?" I say in a little voice.

"Exactly. And do you think I'd have allowed an insignificant thing like the genetics of our child get in the way of our happiness?"

Insignificant?

The warm, soft rug that is his love for me wraps itself closer. Insignificant.

"But you always love the whole breeding thing. Claiming me. Making me yours. I thought—"

"Do you not know why I love that?" he interrupts me.

"Because it's hot?"

"That too," he says wryly. "But I love it because it's a way of saying, we're in this together. That you and I are bonded in the most primal way because you accept me owning you and wanting to protect and love you unconditionally. My love for you has no ifs or buts, Adi. It never has."

I think I might cry with happiness. "Really?"

"My love. My best girl." He pulls me into his arms and we snuggle into the bed covers. "You and our children were always going to be mine. If you had become pregnant by another man, however it had happened, you would *still have been mine*. I couldn't have stopped loving you. I wouldn't love the kids any less. Genetics isn't love, sweetheart. We were lucky you got pregnant so easily, and there were no complications. But if there had, we'd have done whatever was necessary, together. We'd have tried IVF, or we'd have adopted, or even I'd have turkey basted you with Super Sperm if that was what you really wanted."

"Not the turkey baster, surely," I laugh.

His mouth twitches but then he's serious again. "Me breeding you is just about you and me. It's our kinky game, yes, but it's also about our intent to love and be everything for each other. For me to fill you up with love and commitment. What it has *never* been about, is genetics."

I snuggle my face into his neck and whisper, "I'm glad."

He holds me tighter in his arms. "My silly good girl. I can't believe you didn't know that."

"I think I did..." Would we really be together if I had honestly thought he'd have not loved me because I'd had another man's child? No. Rhys is incredibly kind and loving, I didn't really think that. "I just..."

"Needed to hear me say it."

"Yeah." I sigh with contentment. "Is there anything you worry about? Something you need me to say." Since we're on the topic of home truths. But I expect him to brush it off. Say there's nothing and he isn't scared of anything.

"That you'd love me if I wasn't rich," he answers promptly.

I bolt upright. "What?"

He raises one eyebrow. "Relax. I haven't lost any money."

"I know!" The finances are as much my domain as his these days. But how could he think that I was a gold digger? "And I wouldn't care if you had. So long as we could feed and keep our family warm and safe, I wouldn't care."

"My little fiery dragon." He drags me back to his chest. "I didn't doubt you any more than you did me. But sometimes I doubt *me*. You're the best thing that has ever happened to me, Adi so of course when I'm exhausted and worried about ensuring all our employees are secure in their jobs and the businesses are sustainable, the fear that underpins it all is the least justified. That I might lose the person I love most. You."

"You're not going to lose me."

"Fears are just that, Adi. Fears." He presses a kiss to the top of my head. "The money and the genetics, they're just a bonus on top of our love."

"I love you," I whisper as we relax towards sleep.

"I love you too."

THANKS

Thank you for reading, I hope you enjoyed it.

Want to read a little more Happily Ever After? Click to get exclusive epilogues and free stories! or head to EvieRoseAuthor.com

If you have a moment, I'd really appreciate a review wherever you like to talk about books. Reviews, however brief, help readers find stories they'll love.

Love to get the news first? Follow me on your favored social media platform - I love to chat to readers and you get all the latest gossip.

If the newsletter is too much like commitment, I recommend following me on BookBub, where you'll just get new release notifications and deals.

- amazon.com/author/evierose
- bookbub.com/authors/evie-rose
- instagram.com/evieroseauthor
- tiktok.com/@EvieRoseAuthor

INSTALOVE BY EVIE ROSE

Stalker Kingpins

Spoiled by my Stalker

From the moment we lock eyes, I'm his lucky girl... But there's a price to pay

Owned by her Enemy

I didn't expect the ruthless new kingpin—an older man, gorgeous and hard—to extract such a price for a ceasefire: an arranged marriage.

His Public Claim

My innocence is up for auction, sold to the highest bidder.

Pregnant by the Mafia Boss

Kingpin's Baby

I beg the Kingpin for help... And he offers marriage.

Baby Proposal

My boss walked in on me buying "magic juice" online... And now he's demanding to be my baby's daddy!

Grumpy Bosses

Older Hotter Grumpier

My billionaire boss catches me reading when I should be

working. And the punishment...?

London Mafia Bosses

Captured by the Mafia Boss

I might be an innocent runaway, but I'm at my friend's funeral to avenge her murder by the mafia boss: King.

Taken by the Kingpin

Tall, dark, older and dangerous, I shouldn't want him.

Stolen by the Mafia King

I didn't know he has been watching me all this time.

I had a plan to escape. Everything is going perfectly at my wedding rehearsal dinner until *he* turns up.

Caught by the Kingpin

The kingpin growls a warning that I shouldn't try his patience by attempting to escape.

There's no way I'm staying as his little prisoner.

Claimed by the Mobster

I'm in love with my ex-boyfriend's dad: a dangerous and powerful mafia boss twice my age.

Snatched by the Bratva

I have an excruciating crush on this man who comes into the coffee shop. Every day. He's older, gorgeous, perfectly dressed. He has a Russian accent and silver eyes.

Kidnapped by the Mafia Boss

I locked myself in the bathroom when my date pulled out a knife. Then a tall dark rescuer crashed through the door… and kidnapped me.

Held by the Bratva

"Who hurt you?"

Before I know it, my gorgeous neighbour has scooped me up into his arms and taken me to his penthouse. And he won't let me go.

Filthy Scottish Kingpins

Forbidden Appeal

He's older and rich, and my teenage crush re-surfaces as I beg the former kingpin to help me escape a mafia arranged marriage. He stares at me like I'm a temptress he wants to banish, but we're snowed in at his Scottish castle.

Captive Desires

I was sent to kill him, but he's captured me, and I'm at his mercy. He says he'll let me go if I beg him to take his…

Printed in Dunstable, United Kingdom